The
Nevada
Nightmare
Novel

Here's what readers from around the country are saying about Johnathan Rand's AMERICAN CHILLERS:

"MISSISSIPPI MEGALODON was awesome! You're the best writer in the WORLD!"

-Julian T., age 8, Florida

"American Chillers is the best book series in the world! I love them!"

-Anneliese B., age 10, Michigan

"I'm reading FLORIDA FOG PHANTOMS, and it's great! When are you going to write a book about Utah?"

-David H., Age 7, Utah

"MISSISSIPPI MEGALODON is so rad! Where in the world do you get these ideas? You are the awesomest author ever!"

-Eli L., Age 9, Illinois

"I read DANGEROUS DOLLS OF DELAWARE and it was super creepy. My favorite book is POLTERGEISTS OF PETOSKEY. You make me like to read even more!"

-Brendon P., Age 8, Michigan

"I love your books! I just finished SINISTER SPIDERS OF SAGINAW. It really freaked me out! Now I'm reading MIS-SISSIPPI MEGALODON. It's really good. Can you come to our school?"

-Blane B., age 11, Indiana

"I'm your biggest fan in the world! I just started your DOUBLE THRILLERS and it's great!"

-Curtis J., Age 11, California

"I just read the book: CURSE OF THE CONNECTICUT COYOTES and it really freaked me out when Erica thought she got attacked by a coyote!"

-Shaina B., Age 10, Minnesota

"I love your books so much that I read everyone in my school library and public library! I hope I get a chance to come to CHILLERMANIA, and I'm saving my money to make it happen. You rock! Keep writing, and I'm your biggest fan!"

-Makayla B., Age 9, Missouri

"Your books are the best I've ever read in my life! I've read over 20 and double thumbs up to all of them!"

-Justus K., Age 11, California

"I never like to read until I discovered your books. The first one I read was VIRTUAL VAMPIRES OF VERMONT, and it totally freaked me out! Me and my friends have our own American Chillers book club. Will you come to one of our meetings?"

-Carson C., age 12, Oklahoma

"I love the American Chillers series I only have three more books to go! My favorite book is HAUNTING IN NEW HAMPSHIRE. It's awesome!"

-Eriana S., age 10, Ohio

"I've read most of your American Chillers books! My favorite was WISCONSIN WEREWOLVES. Right now I am reading KENTUCKY KOMODO DRAGONS. I love it because it is mystery/adventure/chillers! Thank you for writing such exciting books!"

-Maya R., age 9, Georgia

"When we visited my grandparents in San Diego, I found your books at *The Yellow Book Road* bookstore. I bought one and read it in three days! My grandparents took me back to the bookstore and bought me five more! I can't stop reading them!"

-Amber Y, age 11, Hawaii

"I've read every single one of your Michigan and American Chillers and they're all great! I just finished VICIOUS VACUUMS OF VIRGINIA and I think it's the best one yet! Go Johnathan Rand!"

-Avery R., age 10, Delaware

"Your books are the best ones I've ever read! I tried to write my own, but it's hard! How do you come up with so many great books? Please tell me so I can be a writer, too!"

-Lauren H., age 12, Montana

"My family and I were vacationing in northern Michigan and stopped at CHILLERMANIA and you were there! It was the best day of my life!"

-Andrew T., age 8, Tennessee

Got something cool to say about Johnathan Rand's books? Let us know, and we might publish it right here! Send your short blurb to:

Chiller Blurbs
281 Cool Blurbs Ave.
Topinabee, MI 49791

Other books by Johnathan Rand:

Michigan Chillers:

American Chillers:

Freddie Fernortner, Fearless First Grader:

Adventure Club series:

For Teens:

American Chillers Double Thrillers:

America's #1 Series for MAXIMUM CHILLS!

#31: The Nevada Nightmare Novel

Johnathan Rand

An AudioCraft Publishing, Inc. book

Book storage and warehouses provided by Chillermania!©
Indian River, Michigan

Warehouse security provided by:
Lily Munster, Scooby-Boo, and Spooky Dude

American Chillers #31: The Nevada Nightmare Novel
ISBN 13-digit: 978-1-893699-12-0

Librarians/Media Specialists:
PCIP/MARC records available **free of charge** at
www.americanchillers.com

Cover illustration by Dwayne Harris
Cover layout and design by Sue Harring

Dickinson Press Inc. Grand Rapids, MI USA Job#3938900 October 2011

The
Nevada
Nightmare
Novel

It was a dark and stormy night in Henderson, Nevada.

In my bedroom, I stared at the words on the computer screen and then read them out loud.

"It was a dark and stormy night in Henderson, Nevada."

That was how my story was to begin. It was a homework assignment. Everyone in our class had to write a spooky Halloween story, and it had to start with that sentence.

It was a dark and stormy night in Henderson, Nevada.

Why? Because our teacher, Mr. Harper, said that it would help our creativity. He said that all of our stories would be very different and unique, even though each student began the exercise with the same sentence. And Henderson, Nevada is where I live, of course. It's where I go to school. I'm a fifth-grader at Vandenberg Elementary. Henderson is a city about ten miles southeast of Las Vegas, and I think just about everybody's heard of Las Vegas. It's a fun city.

But Henderson is just as much fun. I have a lot of great friends, and there are some great parks nearby, including Discovery Park, which is only a few blocks from where we live. The weather gets really hot in the summer, but it cools off during the winter months. Still, we don't get any snow, because it doesn't get cold enough. Sometimes, I wish we would have a snowstorm. I think it would be fun to build a snowman or have a snowball fight with my friends.

But I couldn't think about that right now. Right now, I had to think about my homework assignment, which was to write a story. I already had the first sentence, of course, but I didn't know what to write about after that.

A ghost story? I thought. *A haunted house? A boy wizard? A fantasy world filled with dragons?* I had so many options, so many directions I could go, but I found it confusing to even begin. Mr. Harper had told us that writing a book, even a short story, can be difficult. He told us to work hard, but let our imaginations guide us.

Well, my imagination wasn't guiding me anywhere. I just sat at the desk in my bedroom, staring at the computer screen, which was blank except for that single, short phrase. The little black cursor taunted me as it blinked at the end of the sentence.

It was a dark and stormy night in Henderson, Nevada.

But the weird part? It really was a dark and stormy night. It was October, and a chilly wind was blowing, rain was falling, and lightning had been flashing for the past couple of hours. One thunderclap was so loud that it shook the entire house.

My sister, Hannah, came to my bedroom door. "Devon," she said, "Mom says to turn off your computer until the storm passes."

"Tell her I will," I said.

Using the mouse, I moved the cursor to shut down the computer, but it was too late. A sudden, bright flash lit up my bedroom, and at the exact same time, an enormous thunderclap exploded. Simultaneously, my bedroom light went out, and sparks shot out of the electrical outlets!

The power came back on several hours later. Lightning had struck an electrical transformer in front of our house, causing a strong power surge and knocking out power for several blocks.

But the really bad news?

The surge of electricity fried a bunch of our household appliances, including the stereo, microwave, television . . . and my computer. Dad said that he was sure our insurance would pay to have everything replaced, but that didn't help me at the moment. I really needed to get started on my story for school, but now I had nothing to write with. The computer in my bedroom was the only one in the house, except for my dad's laptop, which is only for his job. Even though it was a little old and I couldn't use it to play any games, I could still use it for my homework assignments.

"I guess you're just going to have to write your story the old-fashioned way," Mom said.

"How's that?" I asked.

"With a pen and paper," she replied.

I frowned. I was okay with writing on paper, but I was getting faster and faster on the computer keyboard. I liked the feeling of the keys under my fingers, and I liked the way the letters and words came out all neat and crisp when I printed my story.

But I had two weeks before the story needed to be handed in, so I had plenty of time. I could always use a computer at school or at the public library if I needed to. And besides: the story didn't have to be very long. Mr. Harper had told us to keep it around three pages.

But I was still stuck.

What am I going to write about? I thought, as I lay back in bed. I wanted my story to be different from everyone else's. I knew that most of my classmates would be writing about ghosts or haunted houses or vampires, and there was nothing wrong with that.

But I really want my story to be different, I thought. *What can I write that would be different, and really, really great?*

As it would turn out, I wouldn't have to worry about getting an idea for a really great story. What I would have to worry about was a nightmare. Not something in my sleep, but a real, living nightmare that came to me while I was awake.

The most horrifying part? I had no control over the nightmare . . . and that's why things got way out of hand.

3

The morning after the storm, Hannah and I rode our bikes around the block to see what other damage had been done. All over the neighborhood, broken branches and limbs littered yards. One enormous branch landed on someone's car. The hood had a big dent in it, and the windshield was smashed. We saw a few trucks that belonged to the power company, their yellow lights flashing.

"We were lucky we didn't get a tornado," Hannah said. "This is bad enough as it is."

Looping around the next block, we saw a man tacking an orange cardboard sign to an electrical pole. When he was finished, he backed off, inspected his work, and then walked away.

"Garage sale," Hannah said, reading the sign out loud. "15897 Bobtail Circle. Saturday and Sunday only."

"Want to go?" I asked. "It's only a couple blocks away."

"Sure," Hannah replied.

I like going to garage sales. Sometimes, you can find some really cool stuff. Last summer at a garage sale, I found a box of comic books for two dollars! I couldn't believe it. I looked on the Internet, and some of the older comics were worth as much as ten dollars. I didn't sell them, though. I figured the longer I kept them, the more valuable they would be. Maybe they would be worth a fortune when I got older.

We continued riding our bikes along the sidewalk. In several places, we had to swerve around tree branches that had fallen.

After rounding a corner, we came to a big tree that had been blown down by the wind. It was blocking our way, so we slowed, and I looked behind us.

"There aren't any cars coming," I said. "Let's go around."

We carefully rode into the empty street, and I looked over my shoulder again, just to be sure there weren't any vehicles coming from behind us.

Unfortunately, the tree was blocking our view of the driveway in front of us, and we had no idea there was a truck backing out at that very moment. By the time we did realize it, it was too late for the driver to see us.

4

Hannah screamed. We hadn't been traveling very fast, and that's what saved us both from getting hit by the truck. Our brakes shrieked as our bikes came to a halt only inches from the vehicle.

The driver, hearing Hannah scream, stomped on the brakes and his vehicle jerked to a halt. He got out and hurried around to the back of the truck. He looked panicky and scared. His eyes were wide.

"Are you kids all right?" he asked.

"Yeah," Hannah said. "We didn't see you."

"I didn't see you, either," the man said. "Not with that big tree in the way. You sure you're both all right?"

"We're fine," Hannah said.

"Yeah, me, too," I echoed.

"Okay," the man said with a smile. "That storm sure was a doozy, wasn't it?"

"It sure was," I replied.

The man got back into his truck and waited for us to pass.

"That was close," Hannah said as we rode back onto the sidewalk and continued down the block.

Up ahead, we saw another orange sign for the garage sale. A dark arrow, pointing to the left, was beneath it.

"There it is," I said, and we coasted to a stop at the edge of the driveway.

A few cars lined the street, and a few people were milling about in the driveway. There was a two-car garage attached to the house, and the door had been rolled up. Three big folding tables were cluttered with all sorts of things: old compact discs, shoes, clothes, games, lamps, tools, and more.

Hannah leaned close to me. *"These people must've been saving this stuff for years,"* she whispered. *"How did they fit all this junk in their house?"*

I snickered. There really was a lot of stuff, and it didn't look like it would all fit into the garage and the house put together.

"Feel free to look around," a man said, and I recognized him as the guy who had put up the sign.

"Thanks," I replied.

Hannah and I wandered around the tables, looking for anything interesting. Most of what we saw seemed like just a lot of old junk. Still, some people found things they thought would be useful, and they carried various items as they wandered around the tables.

Hannah was looking at some collectible dolls. I walked into the garage, where more tables were set up. On the far wall was a big bookshelf filled with paperbacks. A handwritten sign read: All books: 25¢ each.

Can't beat that, I thought, and I walked to the shelf. I love to read, and I thought I might find a book that I'd like.

There were a lot of westerns, which I didn't really care for. And romance books. Yuck. I found a science fiction book that looked cool, along with another book about fog phantoms in Florida. That one looked pretty creepy.

I was just about to dig into my pocket to find fifty cents to pay for the two books when another book caught my eye. It was hardbound, and it looked old. There was no title on the spine or on the cover.

I picked it up, unaware that I was about to make a terrifying discovery that would turn my world upside down.

5

The strange thing about the book was that there was no writing inside. Nothing. No words, no letters, no numbers, nothing. It appeared to be some sort of old notebook that no one had ever used. Still, it looked pretty cool, and I thought it might be fun to use it to write my own stories.

"What did you find?" Hannah asked as she walked up to me. She, too, had a book in her hand, along with a board game that looked brand new.

"It looks like an old notebook," I said,

handing it to her. She took it in her hands and flipped it over.

"It looks like it's a thousand years old," my sister said. Then, raising it to her face, she sniffed and winced. "It smells old, too."

She handed it back to me, and I, too, sniffed it. It smelled dry and musky, like most old books. Once again, I flipped open the book and turned the pages. Still, I found no writing. The pages were a little yellow from age, but there was nothing written on any of them.

"I think I'm going to buy it," I said. "I think it would be cool to use as a notebook."

Hannah wasn't very interested in the book, and she continued to browse the tables and shelves. I tucked my three books beneath my arm and continued searching the tables and shelves, but I didn't find anything else I was interested in.

I looked around for a few more minutes, and then I carried the three books to the man seated behind a small card table. I reached into my pocket to get my money.

"Found some treasures, did you?" the man said with a smile.

"Yeah, just these books," I replied.

"Reading is good for you," the man said. "Good brain food." He opened his cashbox containing paper money and a handful of change. "You even found that old notebook that's been kicking around here for a few years," he said.

"How old is it?" I asked.

The man shook his head. "Got no idea," he answered. "Not even sure where it came from."

I picked up the old book and held it in my hands. I had to admit: I was strangely fascinated by it. I wondered if it might be valuable. Once, I heard about a woman who bought a painting at a flea market for one dollar, only to find out that it was an authentic portrait painted by some famous artist. It turned out to be worth nearly a half million dollars!

Then again, if the old book I found was worth a lot of money, the man probably wouldn't be selling it at his garage sale.

"Seventy-five cents?" I asked.

"That's right," the man said.

I handed him a dollar, and he dropped a quarter in my palm.

"Enjoy your books," the man said.

"Oh, I'm sure I will," I replied. "I love to read."

I carried the books to my bicycle. Hannah had already paid for her book and game and was waiting for me, staring up at the gray sky.

"It looks like it might rain again," she said.

"It better not," I replied. "Not until we get home. I don't want my books to get wet."

We left the garage sale and headed for home, riding our bikes along the sidewalk. I held my books under my left arm and steered with my right.

And I wondered about the old book. I wondered why no one had written anything in it. Usually, if someone buys a notebook, they write in it. They keep a diary or journal, or they write a story.

Maybe whoever bought it all those years ago never got around to writing a story, I thought. *Maybe they bought it and then forgot about it. Maybe they lost it.*

Either way, I was looking forward to using it. I already knew what I was going to write. I was going to use my new notebook to write the story for my school project. Mr. Harper would probably think that it was cool when I turned in my story written in a book that was probably one hundred years old or more.

If I ever come up with a story, I thought. So far, all I had was the very first line.

It was a dark and stormy night in Henderson, Nevada.

I needn't have worried. I'd get an idea for a very creepy story, all right. A creepy story that, within twenty-four hours, would turn into a real, live nightmare.

At home, I showed my books to my mom. She, too, was very interested in the old notebook.

"The cover looks like it's made out of leather," Mom said as she turned the book over in her hands. Then, she opened it and flipped through the pages.

"See?" I said. "There's no writing in it at all. Not even any lines or numbers."

"It looks like it was made to be someone's old journal or diary," Mom said as she handed the book back to me. "Back in the old days, most people wrote things down because they had no other way of recording or taking pictures of things that they wanted to share or remember."

Thunder rumbled in the distance. My sister had been right: it started to rain again. Thankfully, we'd made it home before it started. Hannah was now in the living room, watching a television show.

As for me, I thought it was the perfect time to get started on my story. I carried my books to my bedroom, closed the door, and climbed onto my bed. First, I flipped through the science fiction book. It looked pretty exciting, and I couldn't wait to read it. The fog phantoms book looked pretty good, too. Then, I put those two books aside and picked up the old notebook. There was a pencil on the nightstand beside my bed, and I picked it up.

Carefully, I wrote the first sentence of my story on the first page.

It was a dark and stormy night in Henderson, Nevada.

Then, I closed my eyes and started thinking.

Vampires? Ghosts? A haunted house? Zombies? Monsters?

Those were all good ideas, but I was sure a lot of my classmates would be writing about those things. I wanted to do something different, something unique and original.

And that's when something really strange began to happen. . . .

7

I opened my eyes and stared at the old book in my hands. I felt the dry, yellow pages with my index finger.

But here was the strange part:

Things—pictures—began to appear in my mind. It was as if my imagination was becoming a movie in my brain. I closed my eyes once again and saw shapes and forms appearing in the darkness. At first, these forms were just large, blotchy objects. But as they began to move about,

I noticed they were taking shape. Not only that, they were also changing colors. A dark blue dragon suddenly appeared, its vast, leathery wings flapping in the darkness. I knew it was just my imagination, but the scene was very vivid, very clear, and when the dragon issued a burst of fire from its mouth, I jumped. I could actually feel the heat of the yellow flame whirling in the darkness before me.

Suddenly, another dragon appeared. This one was a deep red, a rich, coppery color, and it drew the attention of the dark blue dragon. I watched in strange fascination as the two dragons battled one another on the dark screen before my eyes. I say 'screen,' because that's what it was like: it was as if I was watching the events unfold on some giant, three-dimensional television screen in my imagination. I could hear sounds, too. The dragons were squealing and screeching, and their wings beat the black air as they whirled about, locked in battle.

The really crazy thing, however, was how

real it was. What I was seeing was much more vivid than a dream, much clearer than anything I could've imagined on my own.

But, of course, I'm imagining it on my own, I thought. I'm only seeing the dragons in my imagination.

I watched, eyes closed, fascinated. I was no longer aware of my surroundings. I completely forgot about the old notebook in my hands. It was as if I was lost in another world, focused only on the two dragons as they fought one another in the blackness of my mind.

Then, I wondered something else: if it's only my imagination, maybe I can create something. Maybe if I think about something else, it will appear.

Fire spewed from the dragons' mouths as they continued to fight, their squeals and snarls louder than ever.

A snake.

That's what I thought of. A big, coiled cobra, its hood spread wide, swaying methodically

39

back-and-forth, ready to strike.

And it appeared!

In my mind, in the darkness, while the dragons fought, the cobra appeared. It was much closer to me than the dragons were, and if it hadn't been part of my imagination, I would've been completely freaked out. Everything about the snake looked real.

But what happened next, unfortunately, was also real. The snake bobbed back and forth, slowly, methodically. Without warning, it lunged forward, opened its mouth, and clamped onto my leg with its powerful jaws. I felt its two needle-like teeth pierce my skin and felt the hot, deadly venom pouring into my bloodstream. This was not my imagination. The pain was as real as anything I'd ever felt, and all I could do was scream as the snake sank his teeth deeper and deeper into my flesh.

I opened my eyes and tried to pull my leg away from the attacking cobra . . . which wasn't a cobra at all. It was—

Hannah.

Her hand was on my leg, and she yanked it away, horrified. I don't know who was more scared: her or me. Her eyes were wide, and her mouth hung open as if she was about to scream.

"What did you do that for?!?!" I snapped.

"Didn't you hear me calling for you?"

I shook my head. "No," I replied.

"You didn't hear me knocking on your door?" Hannah asked.

Again, I shook my head. "No," I said.

"Were you asleep?"

"No, I was—"

Just what had I been doing? I wondered. I thought I had been imagining those dragons and the snake. If that had been the case, I still would've heard Hannah calling for me or knocking on my bedroom door.

"You were what?" Hannah prodded.

"You're asking a lot of questions," I said. "What do you want, anyway?"

"Dinner is ready," Hannah said. "Mom's been calling for you. When you didn't answer, she asked me to come and get you."

I understood what she was saying, but her words just seemed to bounce around in my head without meaning. I was too focused on what had just happened, on the dragons and the snake in my imagination.

Was that it? I wondered. *Had I somehow fallen asleep?*

No. I couldn't have fallen asleep that fast. It just wasn't possible, at least not for me.

"Well, you'd better hurry up," Hannah said. "Your dinner is getting cold." Then, she left the bedroom.

I swung my legs off the bed. I was still holding the open book in my hands, and my fingers were still touching the paper. I closed it, placed it on the bed, and stood. The smells of dinner—grilled hamburgers, potatoes, and green beans—drifted through my open bedroom door.

I strode into the hall, through the living room, and into the kitchen. Mom, Dad, and Hannah were already seated at the table.

"Hey, sleepyhead," Mom said with a smile. "If you would've slept any longer, you would've missed dinner."

I shook my head as I took my place at the table. "I wasn't sleeping," I said. "I just had the weirdest thing happen to me. I was—"

I stopped speaking, lost in thought.

"Cat got your tongue?" Dad asked as he handed me a plate of juicy hamburgers. Using my fork, I stabbed a patty and dropped it on the bun on my plate. My eyes scanned the table, searching for the ketchup and mustard. I found both plastic bottles and began decorating my burger.

"I was working on ideas for my story," I continued. "I guess my imagination kind of went wild for a couple of minutes."

"He completely freaked out when I grabbed his leg," Hannah said.

I smiled. "That's only because I was thinking about a giant cobra at that very moment," I said. "It was really weird. In my mind, I saw the cobra attack me. When Hannah grabbed my leg, it was at the exact same moment that the cobra struck."

Mom smiled. "You and your imagination," she said.

"It's going to get you into trouble one of these days," Hannah warned.

"It will not," I said with a frown.

But as it would turn out, my sister was right. My imagination was about to get us all into big, big trouble.

Later that night:

I have a desk in the corner of my bedroom. It's made out of wood, and I use it mostly for doing my homework. There's a lamp on it, some books, and a plastic cup filled with pens and pencils.

And tonight there were two new items on it: the old notebook I bought at the garage sale and a piece of paper. I had been sitting at my desk for half an hour, doodling on the paper. I was drawing fire-breathing dragons and a big cobra snake. My intention was to sit down and think about the story I needed to write, but when no ideas came to me, I became distracted and started to draw.

I'm never going to get this story finished if I don't get started writing, I thought.

I pushed the paper to the side and opened the notebook. I stared at the first line.

It was a dark and stormy night in Henderson, Nevada.

Suddenly, an incredible thing happened. From nowhere, I was struck with an idea that was so scary, so cool, and so creepy. In my mind, I saw the entire story unfold from beginning to end. I saw the characters, the places, the scenes. I knew the plot, I knew the ending. It all came to me in what seemed like a split second. Excitement raced through my veins.

That's it! I thought. *This is the best story idea ever!*

Quickly, I began to write. I wrote furiously, much faster than I normally write. I tried not to be too sloppy, but I wanted to make sure I got my entire story written before I forgot it. In the process, I made a few mistakes, but I didn't worry about them. I knew that I would go back and revise my story several times before I finished. I just concentrated on getting my ideas down on paper. I wrote and wrote and wrote and wrote, never suspecting in a million years that what I was writing was about to come to life.

10

It wasn't too long before I heard a knock on my door. It creaked open a little, and Mom's face appeared.

"Hey, Sport," she said. "Time to brush your teeth and hit the sack."

"But I can't, Mom!" I pleaded. "I'm not done with my story."

"How close are you?"

"I'm almost finished," I begged. "Can I please stay up long enough to finish it?"

Mom frowned. "How long do you think it will take you?"

I looked at the digital clock on my desk. It was eight-thirty.

"I think I'll be finished by nine," I said. "Please?"

"Tell you what," Mom said. "Brush your teeth, get your pajamas on, and then you can finish the story. But you've got to be in bed by nine, regardless of whether you finish your story or not. Tomorrow is a school day."

I put down my pencil and stood. It was hard to drag myself away from the desk, as I was afraid I would forget how my story ended. I know that might sound silly, but I've lost good ideas before. Mr. Harper always tells us to write down our ideas so we don't forget them. I certainly didn't want that to happen with the story I was working on.

So, I didn't waste any time. After brushing my teeth, I changed into my pajamas and returned to my desk. I picked up my pencil and continued my story, writing as fast as I could, glancing at the digital clock every few minutes.

Finally, at exactly eight fifty-eight, I finished. I let out a deep breath as I wrote the words The End. Of course, I knew I wasn't completely finished. I would have to go back and reread and rewrite the story, fixing any mistakes I might have made, doing whatever I could to make my story better. Mr. Harper told us in class that some authors rewrite their stories seven or eight times, or even more.

And that's what I was looking forward to: rewriting. Rewriting my story would give me the opportunity to experience it all over again. The story was good, and it was scary, and I was looking forward to making it even better. In fact, there was no doubt in my mind that I would get an 'A.' I knew Mr. Harper was going to be impressed. He would be impressed with my story, but I knew he would be impressed with my old notebook, too.

I bet it would be cool to be an author and write books for a living, I thought. I would love to spend my days creating strange worlds on paper and giving other people the chance to read about them.

This, of course, was before everything happened, before I learned of the horrifying secret of the old notebook, before my entire world became a living nightmare—a nightmare that began that very night.

11

I finished my story by nine o'clock, just as I thought I would. Mom checked in on me to make sure I was in bed, but I pretended I was asleep. As soon as she closed the door, I pulled my flashlight from beneath my pillow. I kept it hidden there for late night reading.

But that's not what I was going to use it for that night.

I clicked on the flashlight and shined it on the nightstand where my old notebook and pencil sat. I picked them up, sank down on my pillow, pulled the covers over my head, and opened up the notebook to the very beginning. I began to reread my story, looking for spelling mistakes and other errors. I focused on each sentence, thinking about how I could make it better. Sometimes I erased words; sometimes I erased entire sentences. I rewrote an entire paragraph by writing the new sentences above the old ones. Then, I erased the old paragraph, leaving the new one in its place.

It took me nearly an hour to go through my entire story, revising and rewriting as I went. Still, I wasn't finished. I began rereading and rewriting from the very beginning for a second time. I was surprised at the number of mistakes I found, especially because I had already gone over the story once.

But it was a great story. Using the strange experience I had earlier in the day, when the two dragons and the cobra had appeared in my mind like a three-dimensional movie, I created a tale in which I was the main character, along with my family. In my story, a strange thunderstorm rolled through Henderson. The storm brought a pirate ship that sailed through the air. After the storm passed, weird things began to happen. Strange creatures and beings began to appear all through the town. I wrote about the two dragons and the snake, but I also included other things. When I was little, I constantly had nightmares about a weird cartoon-like wolf that chased me. No matter how fast I ran, I was never quick enough. I usually awoke screaming, just as the wolf pounced on me. I made the wolf a villain in my story.

I also added other creatures and characters: a crazed pirate named Redbeard, a maniac knight in shining armor, a small fairy that could sprinkle dust on you and turn you into stone, and a strange, hooded zombie, which was another creature from one of my childhood nightmares.

The problem was, I didn't like the ending. In my story, the creatures arrived with the thunderstorm and the pirate ship, like they were a part of it. But when the storm had passed, the creatures remained to threaten the town, including my family. I became the hero by blowing up all the evil creatures on the pirate ship. That sounded exciting, but it wasn't very original. It seems like every movie I've watched and even a lot of the books that I read end with someone blowing something up.

Which is fine, I guess, but I wanted the end of my story to be different, something that would be surprising to the reader. I could leave it the way it was and probably get a pretty good grade, but I knew I could do better. I just had to think about it.

So that's what I decided to do. I erased the very last page of my story and decided I would sleep on it overnight and think about it for another day or two. I was sure I could come up with a better ending than what I'd already written. All I had to do was try harder. Maybe I'd have a new idea and a better ending by tomorrow morning.

I closed my notebook and placed it, along with my pencil, on my nightstand. Then, I clicked off the flashlight and slipped it beneath my pillow.

The story was probably one of the longest stories I've ever written. I didn't have a title yet, but I was thinking about calling it The Fantasy Storm, or something like that. Regardless of what title I decided upon, I was sure Mr. Harper would like it.

But I hadn't quite finished my story. I hadn't written the perfect ending.

No matter. Because as I was about to find out, my story had a mind of its own. While I was thinking about how I was going to end it, my characters were already thinking about how they were going to end me.

12

Sometime during the night, I was jolted awake by a loud thunderclap. It shook the house, rattled the windows, and caused my bed to tremble. I could hear the wind swirling and roaring around the house. The rain pounded the rooftop. I thought it strange that we'd had two severe storms within a day of each other.

I turned my head and looked at the glowing numbers of my digital alarm clock. It read 4:34.

A flash of lightning lit up my room, and a

split second later, a thunderbolt shook the house again. The rain droning on the roof grew heavier, deafening. It sounded like an entire ocean was pouring down all around and above me.

Slowly, I pulled back the covers and climbed out of bed. I put on my slippers, which padded on the carpet as I walked toward my bedroom window. I reached up, pulled back the drapes a tiny bit, and looked outside. In the light of the street lamps, I saw the trees whipping violently back and forth, their leaves shiny and wet. I saw puddles in our front yard and a river of rainwater washing down the street.

I stared for a moment. While we do get storms—and sometimes they're severe—they don't happen too often. Again, I thought it was odd that we had two severe thunderstorms so close together, only a day apart. Maybe that happens in other cities and states, but we don't get a lot of rain where we live in Henderson. Not compared to other places in the country.

Strange.

I let go of the curtain, and it fell back into place. I turned and was about to go back to bed . . . then I stopped.

Something was wrong.

For some reason, I was just struck with a weird feeling, like—

Like someone was watching me.

I know it sounds silly, but I was actually getting scared. I was really getting creeped out, and I didn't know why I had such a strong feeling that I was being watched.

But I knew it. I knew I was being watched, no matter how bizarre it sounded.

Now, I'm not afraid of monsters under my bed. I'm not afraid of something coming alive in my closet or something hiding behind my bedroom door. Those things used to scare me when I was little.

But not anymore.

No, I was being watched, all right. I could sense it.

So, I tiptoed to the window and stopped.

Slowly, I raised my hand and grasped the curtain.

Outside, the wind and rain continued to assail the house and our neighborhood. Lightning flashed. Thunder boomed.

I pulled open the curtain, farther and farther, until I had a clear view of our front lawn . . . and a clear view of the strange, hooded zombie figure in our yard, looking at me, slowly beckoning me with his skeletal hand. . . .

13

Seeing the horrifying figure standing in my yard scared me so badly that I flinched and let go of the curtain. It closed just as another white-hot lightning bolt tore through the sky and another thunderclap shook the house.

My nightmare has come back, I thought. It'd been years since I'd had the creepy dream about the weird, hooded zombie that stalked my nightmares. I don't know how my mind had imagined him, as I had never seen anything like him before in my life, certainly not in any comic book or television show. He appeared only in my nightmares when I was little. I had thought the dream was gone for good, but here it was again: the same terrifying figure that had tormented my nights years ago.

And that was the problem.

I wasn't dreaming, and I knew it. I didn't bother trying to pinch myself awake, because I knew that what I was seeing was real.

Or was it?

Slowly, I pulled back the curtain once again and peered into the yard.

Rain continued to pour down, frothing at my window, distorting the scene beyond. The wind assaulted the house, and it lashed the trees in our yard into a chaotic frenzy. The street was flooded, and a torrent of rainwater created a fast-flowing stream that rushed at the curb and wound around the tires of parked cars.

The hooded zombie was gone.

Did I really see that? I wondered. My eyes

traveled back and forth, left and right, searching for any sign of the strange hooded figure. I saw nothing. Yet, I was certain of what I had seen: the freakish character from one of my nightmares years ago. But the nightmares gradually went away, and the last time I had thought about the man with the hood was—

My story. My story I had written in the old notebook. I wrote about the character in my story.

But I had written about a lot of other things, too. I'd written about dragons, a pirate, the wolf that had frightened me so badly when I was little, and other things.

You can't write about things and make them come alive.

Another lightning bolt branched across the sky, its jagged fingers spider-webbed out, reaching over the city like a wiry hand. There was another thunderclap. The booming echo quickly faded, but the rain roared on.

Yet, something had changed. Things seemed still and quiet within the house, and I couldn't understand what was happening.

I let go of the curtain and turned, looking around the room.

What is it? I wondered. *What seems so different now?*

I looked at my nightstand, shrouded in darkness.

That's it, I thought. I saw the silhouette of my digital alarm clock; the numbers weren't glowing. The power had been knocked out.

Again, I turned to the window and slowly pulled back the curtain, expecting to see the hooded figure somewhere in the yard, or maybe in the street. I saw no sign of him anywhere.

Had it only been my imagination?

I let go of the curtain, and it fell back into place. Then, I crawled back into bed and pulled the covers up to my chin. With my right hand, I reached under my pillow, comforted by the flashlight that I'd stashed there. We might not have any electricity, but my flashlight would work just fine. Besides: in a few hours, it would be daylight.

By then the power would probably be back on.

I lay there in the darkness, curled on my side with one hand on my flashlight beneath my pillow. I listened to the storm, to the relentless drumming rain and the howling wind whistling around the house and beneath the eaves of the roof and through the branches of the trees. I watched the lightning erupt, creating a glowing outline around my closed window curtain.

These were the things I was watching, the things I was listening to, when all of a sudden I heard another noise altogether.

A creaking sound.

In my bedroom.

Slowly, I turned my head, only to see the dark shadow of the mysterious hooded figure standing next to my bed!

14

I nearly shot out of bed, but I realized there wasn't any place I could go. The hooded figure was only a couple of feet away, and I was certain he would catch me if I tried to run. I was just about to scream for Mom and Dad when the hooded figure spoke.

"Devon? Are you awake?"

Hannah.

What a relief! It was only my sister. It wasn't the hooded zombie, after all.

I relaxed and propped myself up on my elbows. I had never felt so relieved.

"You completely freaked me out," I said. "I didn't know you were there."

"I didn't mean to scare you," Hannah said. "But I was having a nightmare."

"Well," I said angrily, "go tell Mom and Dad. What am I going to do about it?"

"You were in my nightmare," Hannah replied. "It was horrible. We were being chased by two giant dragons."

A trickle of alarm sprang up from somewhere within my body. Two dragons? I thought, recalling the strange vision I had the day before, remembering what I'd written in my story. I'd written about the dragons in my story, describing them as I remembered them from my vision.

"What were the dragons doing?" I asked.

"They were fighting," Hannah said. "They were fighting, until they saw me. When they saw me, they came after me. I ran as fast as I could, and I was able to hide and get away."

"What else happened in your nightmare?" I asked. By now, I was really interested. I pulled my legs out from beneath the covers and sat on the edge of the bed. Hannah's dark form remained in the middle of my bedroom.

"Lots," she said. "But the worst part of it was that it all seemed so real. I mean, I knew I was having a nightmare, but I couldn't wake myself up. I could hear the thunder and the wind and the rain, and I knew we were having a storm, but I still felt trapped in my nightmare. It was awful. Have you ever had anything like that happen to you?"

"No," I replied, shaking my head. "Not really. I've had some bad dreams, but nothing like that. What made you finally wake up?"

"Well," Hannah replied, "I know this is going to sound silly, but in my dream, I saw a pirate ship floating in the sky. It was drifting beneath the storm clouds with lightning swirling all around. And there was a pirate standing at the front of the ship. He laughed like a madman, and that's when

I woke up. I almost screamed."

A pirate and a pirate ship? I wondered. *That was what my story was about!*

"Wait a minute," I said. "You said that I was in your nightmare, too. Where was I?"

"You were being chased by a giant snake," Hannah replied. "But there were other things that I saw. A weird zombie. And a fairy that could sprinkle dust that could turn people into stone. It was the strangest dream I've ever had."

I thought about this. I thought about how strange it was that Hannah had dreamed about some of the characters in the story I had written. Yet, there was no way she would've known what my story was about, as no one had read it yet.

I was freaked out, but I certainly didn't want to worry Hannah any more than she already was. The nightmare had frightened her, and I didn't want to make her any more scared.

"It was just a nightmare," I said. "You're fine. The storm knocked the power out, though. We don't have any electricity."

"There's one more thing," Hannah said. "There's one more thing about my nightmare that I haven't told you about."

I paused, waiting for her to continue. Outside, a flash of lightning lit up the sky, causing the edges of my curtains to blaze brightly. Thunder rumbled. Wind howled. Rain pounded the roof.

"A wolf," she said. "He was awful. Horrible."

A blade of electricity jolted my body. "A wolf?" I said, my voice just above a whisper.

"Yes," Hannah answered. "Except this wolf looked like—"

"—a cartoon?" I interrupted. "A scary cartoon character?"

"Exactly!" Hannah said. "How did you know?"

At that moment, there was an enormous clap of thunder, and my bedroom window shattered. The wind tossed the curtains aside. Glass exploded all around us and clattered to the floor. The curtain tore open.

And on the other side of the window was the

face I had seen in many, many nightmares: the
face of the horrible wolf was staring at us!

15

Whatever had happened up to that point no longer mattered. Nightmares, dreams, and my story in the old notebook were quickly forgotten. Before, things had seemed a little odd, and maybe a little freaky.

Not anymore.

This wasn't a part of our imaginations, something we dreamed up in our heads. Both Hannah and I had experienced these strange occurrences. Most importantly, we both saw my bedroom window shatter, we both were staring at the same horrifying wolf as he glared menacingly back at us from just beyond my bedroom window. No matter how crazy it seemed, no matter what was happening, we were in trouble, and we knew it. We needed help. It was time to get Mom and Dad.

Grabbing my flashlight from beneath my pillow, I leapt up from the bed. "To Mom and Dad's room!" I shouted. "Hurry!"

I clicked on my flashlight, and Hannah and I sprang. In a few steps, we were out of my bedroom and racing down the hall.

We sprinted past Hannah's open bedroom door and rounded the corner at the end of the hall. I half-expected Mom and Dad to be coming out of their room, as they must have heard my bedroom window shatter and would've gotten up to investigate.

We stopped at their open bedroom door, and I knew right away that something was wrong. First of all, Mom and Dad's bedroom door was always closed. Now, it was open.

What's more, no sound came from their bedroom. I was sure they would have heard the crash of my window breaking, as it must have been loud enough to wake them up. Once, I knocked over a glass of water on my nightstand, and it shattered on my bedroom floor. This brought both Mom and Dad running, wondering what was wrong. But the shattering window had been twenty times louder than the water glass exploding on the floor. It should have easily woken them up.

"Mom! Dad!" I yelled. *"Wake up! Something's wrong! There's a wolf trying to get us!"*

No sound came from their bedroom. The only things I could hear were the wind and the rain and the distant rumble of thunder, which seemed oddly loud. Too loud, in fact.

I swept the flashlight beam over the bedroom. Shadows bobbed and bent.

Mom and Dad's bed was empty, and their bedroom window was open. The curtains fluttered madly in the wind. That's why the thunder, rain, and wind were so loud. Their window was open.

"Where are they?" Hannah asked. Her voice was trembling. "Why is the window open in a thunderstorm?"

Thoughts raced through my mind. "They must've gotten up when the power was knocked out," I replied. "They have to be here in the house, somewhere."

"Mom!" Hannah shouted. *"Dad!"*

We listened. I expected to hear a distant voice from somewhere in the house answering us. After all: Mom and Dad wouldn't leave us alone in the middle of the night. Not during a storm, not ever. They had to be here, somewhere.

Yet—

"Let's go look for them," I said. "They're in the house. They have to be."

We turned, just in time to see a shadow in the hall. I was relieved. Mom and Dad had heard us. They had been in the house, all along.

Hannah breathed a sigh of relief as I swept the flashlight beam up the hall. "I'm so glad we found you guys," she said. "Devon's window shattered, and there was a—"

Hannah stopped speaking when she saw the figure in the hallway, slowly approaching us.

Not Mom.

Not Dad.

It was the wolf.

He was coming toward us on his hind legs, stalking us like he would stalk his prey.

And maybe that's all we were to him.

Prey.

And if the sight of the wolf wasn't scary enough, there was another realization that was even worse.

The front and back doors were at the other end of our house.

Which meant—

We were trapped inside our own home.

16

Seeing the beast coming toward us brought back all of the terror and dread I'd experienced in my nightmares. The horror crashed down upon me like a coat of iron, a heavy weight that made my knees weak, made every muscle in my body slacken. For a moment, I thought I was going to crumble to the floor.

The wolf walked upright, on his hind legs like a human, and his face was twisted and distorted, just as I had remembered him from my nightmares. He was horrifying to look at.

And in his paws—

The old notebook.

The one I bought at the garage sale, the one I had used to write my story. He was carrying it in his two front paws. The only difference now was that there was gold lettering on the front. It was glowing faintly, but I couldn't read what it said.

Hannah and I froze in the bedroom doorway. To the left of us was the bathroom, and I thought about running there and slamming the door. But I knew that it wouldn't stop the wolf. He was too big, too strong, and if he wanted to, I was sure he could break down the door.

I also thought about running through Mom and Dad's bedroom and trying to escape out the window. But again, I was certain that the wolf was much faster than we were. It would be impossible for Hannah and me to flee out the open window before the wolf caught us.

The wolf stopped in the hall. Both corners of his mouth turned upward in a horrible, awful grin.

Then, he held out my notebook, but he wasn't about to give it to me.

"Now you will know," he said, and his voice hissed like air escaping from a tire. "Now you will know what it's like to live within the pages of your story, to know that what you write about, whatever your imagination can dream up, can come true. Now you will find out for yourself that sometimes your nightmares are real."

I had only a moment to read the glowing gold letters on the book:

The Nightmare Novel.

A flash of lightning lit up the house for an instant. Thunder cracked.

Then, the wolf opened his mouth wide, showing rows of huge, sharp fangs . . . and came for us.

17

As the wolf lunged, I darted to one side. Hannah darted to the other. But as it turned out, the beast wasn't after us at all. Instead, he dashed past us and into Mom and Dad's bedroom, where he leapt effortlessly out the window and vanished into the stormy night.

Hannah had fallen to the floor, and now she stood up. She was trembling and shaking all over.

"What . . . what was that?" she stammered.

I shook my head. "I don't know," I replied.

But that's not the truth, I thought. *That was the wolf from my nightmare. The wolf from my story.*

Impossible.

"Where are Mom and Dad?" Hannah asked. She was still trembling, standing in the dark hall in her nightgown and her slippers.

"They have to be in the house somewhere," I said. "Maybe they're in the basement."

"Why would they go into the basement?" Hannah asked.

"I don't know," I replied. "But they have to be here somewhere. Mom and Dad wouldn't just leave us like this. Not in the middle of the night, not in the middle of a bad storm."

I looked down the hall, then back toward my parents' bedroom and out their window. There was no sign of the wolf, nothing out of the ordinary. Except, of course, that their window was open and the storm outside raged on.

I reached out and took Hannah's hand in mine. "Come on," I said. "Let's find Mom and

Dad."

Hannah grasped my hand. "I have a really bad feeling about this," she said.

I did, too. I wasn't at all sure what was going on, and I was scared. I think anybody would be frightened if they were in the same situation. The storm itself was bad enough, but seeing the hooded, hideous figure on the lawn and a talking wolf with my notebook made everything even worse. In fact, it made me question my own sanity. Wolves can't talk. They don't carry notebooks, and they don't walk around on their hind legs. It's just not possible.

But it is, I thought. *It's possible in dreams and nightmares.*

As if reading my thoughts, Hannah spoke.

"Are we having a dream?" she asked. "Is this a nightmare that we're both having?"

I shook my head. "No," I said. "There has to be some sort of explanation. Maybe Mom and Dad are playing a joke."

"Mom and Dad wouldn't play a joke that

would scare us like this," my sister said. "Jokes and pranks are one thing, but this is something totally different."

Hannah was right, and I knew it. But I still wouldn't admit what my mind was already trying to tell me. My mind was telling me that the things that were going on were somehow very real, and I had better start thinking about what could possibly happen next, so that we could be prepared for it.

And I knew something else, something I still wasn't ready to admit to myself. Deep down, I knew that my notebook, my story, had something to do with what was going on. I didn't know how, I didn't know why. But there was something about that old notebook that would provide the answers. Why else would a talking wolf steal it off my nightstand and disappear into the night? Of what importance was my notebook to him?

And—

Why did it read *The Nightmare Novel* on the cover? That hadn't been there before.

We plodded down the hall and made our way toward the kitchen, following the beam of my flashlight. When I heard a noise, I stopped. Hannah stopped beside me.

"Did you hear that?" she whispered.

"Yes," I whispered back. Then, speaking louder: "Mom? Dad?"

My voice was answered by silence. The only things we could hear were the rain as it continued to pound the roof above our heads and the wind as it chewed at the house and gnawed at the trees in our yard. Outside, there was another flash, followed by a churning rumble of thunder.

"Mom?" I said again. "Dad?"

A rising tide of fear welled up within me. Hannah's grip on my hand was so tight that she was nearly crushing my fingers.

Then, a gigantic shadow appeared in the kitchen, and it took only a split second to know the shadow wasn't created by either Mom or Dad. It was far too big, far too wide to be anything human.

And before we could run, before we could attempt to get away, a monster appeared in the hall. . . .

18

The dark silhouette that emerged from the kitchen was enormous, a mountainous wall of black. It was quickly obvious that it was a man, but he was so big that he had to bend over so his head didn't hit the ceiling. He moved slowly and stopped in the middle of the hall.

Hannah squeezed my hand, and I thought my fingers were going to break. I squeezed back.

Slowly, I raised the flashlight beam. I saw two enormous boots in the middle of the hallway.

Raising the beam farther up, I could make out a pair of pants that were made of old cloth or burlap of some sort. At his waist was a huge, gold belt buckle that shined in the flashlight beam. I continued raising my arm ever so slowly, and the white beam illuminated his chest, arms, and shoulders. Finally, I shined the beam into his face.

Without warning, the man raised his gigantic arms and displayed his huge hands, shielding his eyes from the light.

"Hey!" he said. "Knock it off! You're blinding me with that thing!" His voice was deep and rough, and it sounded like he had some sort of accent, although I couldn't really tell exactly what kind it was. Still, he spoke English, and I could understand him easily enough.

"Sorry," I said, and I suddenly felt very silly. There was a giant man in our home—an intruder—and I was apologizing for shining the flashlight in his eyes. We should have been running to get away.

And yet, after the giant man had spoken, I

wasn't as afraid as I had been. If he had wanted to hurt or harm us, he could have. But he didn't. He just stood there with his hands in front of his face and his head turned to the side.

I lowered the flashlight beam to his chest, and he dropped his hands and turned to face us. He was, indeed, a man. An enormous man for sure, but he was human, and not a monster like I'd first thought. He had a thick beard and mustache and dark hair.

Hannah took a step backward, but I remained where I was, holding her hand, aiming the flashlight beam at the giant's chest. I don't think I've ever been more confused or frightened in my life.

"Who . . . who are you?" I managed to stammer.

The towering giant looked at me as if I had asked a ridiculous question. Then, he lowered his hands and spoke.

"You know very well who I am," he replied in his deep booming voice. "If it wasn't for you, I wouldn't be here."

"What do you mean?" I asked. "How did you get into our house?"

"You were the one who dared write in The Nightmare Novel," he replied. "Surely, you must have known what you were doing."

I thought about the old notebook that I bought at the garage sale and how I had used it to write my story.

"I'm not sure I know what you mean," I replied. "All I did was buy that old notebook for a quarter. I had an idea for a story, so I wrote it down. That's all I did. It was just a story for my school assignment."

The giant in the hallway shook his head. "Terrific," he said, rolling his eyes. "Another lame brain that has no idea what he's done."

Lame brain? I thought. Why would he call me that?

Behind me, Hannah tried to draw away. *"Let's get out of here,"* she whispered. *"Let's find Mom and Dad."*

The giant heard her and chuckled. "Oh, I'm afraid that's not possible," he said. "Your parents are gone."

Lightning flashed outside, creating a flash that illuminated the inside of our house. It was followed by an angry crash of thunder.

"Gone?" I said. "What do you mean?"

"Gone as gone can be," the giant replied. "Old Redbeard the pirate took them."

"But that's not possible," I said. "Redbeard is just a character in my story."

"Oh, he's more than that," the giant replied. "He's very, very real, and he has taken your parents."

"But where did he take them?" I asked.

The giant shrugged. "Beats me," he said. "Old Redbeard can do whatever he wants, now that you've brought him to life. He'll probably—"

The giant was interrupted by a haunting, throaty laugh from outside. We could hear it all through the house, but it was most clear coming from down the hall, from my parents' bedroom, from their open window.

"Ah," the giant said. "There he is now. I guess he's still around after all."

Still holding Hannah's hand, I turned and ran down the hall, pulling my sister behind me. We dashed through Mom and Dad's bedroom and peered out the window at one of the most amazing—and horrifying—scenes I have ever witnessed.

19

Outside, the storm continued to rage. The flooded street was now a raging river that showed no sign of diminishing. In fact, it looked as if the water was getting even deeper. Wind licked the trees, and the rain continued to pour down.

But that's not what was so horrifying. What was so horrifying—and unbelievable—was an old pirate ship sailing through the air, just as if it were sailing in the water! It drifted above the rooftops, rocking back and forth in the gale. Its sails were filled with wind and they billowed out, moving the ship along. It floated as effortlessly as a helium balloon, carried through the air by the power of the thunderstorm.

It's my story, I thought. *My story has come to life!*

Hannah drew a breath, and she raised both hands to her mouth to stifle a scream.

"That's him, all right," the giant said from behind us. He had followed us into Mom and Dad's bedroom and was now standing over us, peering out the window, looking at the ancient pirate ship as it lumbered along in the air, swaying to and fro in the powerful gale.

"What's happening?" I asked, and my voice sounded confused, desperate.

"Your story," the giant replied. "You are now living within the reality of the story you wrote."

"But that's not possible," I replied. "It's just a story. It was only my imagination."

The giant shook his head. "Maybe it was just a story," he said, "and maybe it was all from your imagination, in your mind. But you wrote it in The Nightmare Novel. All the characters you wrote about in the book are now alive."

"What is he talking about?" my sister asked. I ignored her, as I was too confused by what the giant had told me.

How could the creatures in my story come alive? I thought. They were just creatures in my head, things I have dreamed up or remembered from old nightmares.

"Oh, it happens, it happens," the giant said as if reading my thoughts. "Every few hundred years, someone seems to find The Nightmare Novel. They don't have any idea what it is. They write down a story, or document their life, and wind up getting into all sorts of trouble. I remember one time, a man wrote a diary of his life and had no idea that he actually created a double of himself, and a double of all of the people he wrote about. It was a horrible mess."

I was shocked. I had never even heard about anything like *The Nightmare Novel* or knew anything like it even existed.

"So, you're telling me that my story has come to life? Everything I've written about has come true?"

The giant shook his head. "Not your story," he replied. "The characters. Now that you've written about them in The Nightmare Novel, they have all come to life."

"What is he saying?" Hannah asked.

"Just what I meant to say," the giant replied to my sister. "Every character your brother wrote about in The Nightmare Novel has come alive. They have minds of their own."

"I'm dreaming," Hannah replied. "There is no way that this is happening."

Outside, a sudden, heavy gust of wind caused the pirate ship to sway. Over the roaring wind and the rumbling thunder, we could hear the creeks and moans of the ancient vessel as it floated through the air. It was the strangest scene I have ever seen in my life.

But then came another sound.

A shout. Then a scream.

Suddenly, a figure appeared on the pirate ship, leaning over the side, leering down at us. He had a long, thick, red beard and was wearing a black pirate hat with a white skull and crossbones on it. He had a black patch covering one eye. He was, unmistakably, the pirate I had created in my story.

Redbeard.

He laughed, and his deep, raspy voice made my skin crawl. His voice boomed over the neighborhood, snarling like the thunder that boiled within the storm clouds.

Then, to my horror, Mom and Dad appeared next to him. Through the sheets of rain, I couldn't see them very well, but it looked as if they had their hands tied behind their backs. They had been kidnapped and were now prisoners on Redbeard's ship.

And I could clearly make out the expressions of horror on their faces.

"Just in time, mateys!" drawled Redbeard.

"Now you can watch these land lubbers walk the plank!"

Oh, no! He was going to make Mom and Dad go overboard, off the side of the ship! They would never survive the fall!

20

"We've got to do something!" I shouted. "That's my mom and dad up there! That nutcase is going to make them walk the plank!"

"Yeah," the giant said. "I think you outdid yourself when you created that character. Redbeard is one nasty fellow. "

"But I didn't mean to!" I said. "I thought it was just a story!"

Hannah began to cry, but the only thing I could do was squeeze her hand. I didn't tell her that everything was going to be okay, because I wasn't so sure myself.

"What can we do?" I asked as I looked up at Redbeard and the terror-stricken faces of my parents.

"The only thing you can do," the giant replied. "You have to destroy your story. You have to erase it from the pages of The Nightmare Novel. That's the only way to get rid of the creatures."

"But that's impossible," I replied. "The wolf stole it. I have no idea where he went."

Above us, the pirate ship continued to sail above the rooftops. It was moving farther and farther away with every passing second. However, my parents had vanished, and all I could see was the nasty face of Redbeard glaring down at us.

"Just kidding about the plank," the pirate snarled loudly. "I think I'll keep them with me. They might come in handy."

Hannah continued to cry, and I continued to plead with the giant.

"There must be something else I can do!" I

said. "Can we stop him?"

The giant shrugged, as if this whole situation didn't seem to bother him at all. He didn't seem worried in the least.

"No, not really," he replied. "If you can't erase your story, then there's nothing you can do. Sorry."

The pirate ship had reached the end of the block. I could no longer see Redbeard or Mom and Dad on board, and the huge ship appeared to be empty, sailing off into the dark, stormy night sky. The scene was oddly familiar; it was identical to what I'd created in my imagination, what I'd written in the pages of *The Nightmare Novel*.

"But there must be something I can do!" I pleaded.

The giant shook his head. "If you don't have The Nightmare Novel, I'm afraid nothing can be done."

"Well, we have to find it," I said. "We can't let that pirate dude sail away with Mom and Dad."

"Where did you have it last?" the giant

asked.

"It was in my room on my nightstand," I replied. "The wolf stole it and ran off with it."

My sister had finally stopped crying. Still, she looked very afraid and confused. I couldn't blame her. I was just as afraid and confused as she was.

The three of us could only look through the broken window and watch as the giant pirate ship sailed through the air and vanished in the darkness.

"We have to find that book," I said. "We have to find where that wolf went and get The Nightmare Novel back if we ever want to see Mom and Dad again."

"Yes, that's the only way," the giant said. He didn't seem worried in the least. "I'm sure the wolf has rejoined his companions on the ship."

"Will you help us?" I asked. I felt a little silly asking for help from someone I didn't even know, and from a giant, too. Yet, I had no other choice. I had to trust him. Besides: he seemed to know a lot about what was going on. He seemed to know how and why the creatures in my story had come alive because I had written about them in *The Nightmare Novel.*

The giant rolled his eyes and shrugged.

"Here we go again," he said. "Why is it that everyone who writes in The Nightmare Novel gets themselves into trouble?"

"Hey," my sister snapped. "Drop the attitude. We need help, like my brother said."

I turned and looked at my sister, surprised at her angry outburst. But I said nothing.

"I'll help," the giant finally said. "But you have to do everything that I tell you."

"And what if we don't?" my sister asked. Again, I was surprised by her anger. A few minutes ago, she had been crying, and now she was mad.

"If you don't do exactly as I say," the giant replied, "you will never see your mother and father again. The Nightmare Novel is very, very powerful. You have created a world of your imagination without considering the consequences. Like others who have used The Nightmare Novel, you have no idea what you have unleashed upon the world around you. You are now trapped within the realm you have created."

I stared up into the dark sky, at the shadows of dark clouds roiling and boiling, at the lightning bolts that flashed over the city. I wondered how I had gotten myself into such a horrible situation, not realizing that the real nightmare hadn't even begun.

21

We stared out the window for a few more moments before the giant finally spoke again.

"Well," he began, "you know nothing of The Nightmare Novel, so that's where I'll begin. You'll need to know its history, its life force, to understand what has happened and why."

"But won't that take a lot of time?" I asked.

The giant shook his head. "I will tell you only what you need to know, and that won't take long at all. But you must listen carefully, for you must understand everything about the book. When you do, you will understand what has happened."

"But who are you?" my sister asked.

"I am called Rollo the Giant," the giant said as he took a bow. "At your service."

"But I didn't create you in my story," I said. "Where did you come from?"

"I am the keeper of The Nightmare Novel," Rollo replied. "I live within its pages, and I am the guardian of its magic."

This was getting more and more confusing with every second. *A giant? The Nightmare Novel? The guardian of its magic?* I thought.

Rollo the Giant began to explain, and Hannah and I listened closely to every word. He told us that the ancient book was created by a wizard long ago. Even the wizard didn't understand the full power of the book he had created, but he knew if it fell into the wrong hands, the results would be horrible. People could use it for their own gain, taking over countries and even the entire world. So, the wizard created Rollo the Giant to look after the book, so that if it ever became lost, Rollo could see to it that whoever had the book in their possession would use it responsibly.

"But where do you live?" I asked.

"I live within the pages of The Nightmare Novel, just like I told you," Rollo replied, very matter-of-factly. "Where else would I live?"

"But that doesn't make any sense," my sister replied. "How do you live inside the pages of a book?"

"You wouldn't understand," the giant replied, "because you're from a different world. Your world is based in reality, while my world is based in magic and dreams. But we'd better stop talking about it, and start to do something. We need to find that book, and find it fast."

Something told me that I was not going to like what Rollo the Giant was going to tell us. Something told me that it would be dangerous, and it would lead to a lot of trouble.

And I was right.

22

I couldn't believe what we were doing.

The first thing Rollo told us we needed to do was to find the pirate ship, so we set out in the pouring rain while lightning streaked across the sky and thunder boomed. I know going out in a thunderstorm isn't the smartest thing to do, but we had no choice. Rollo told us that we had to track down the pirate ship and somehow climb aboard.

And I was glad we had our slippers on, too. Sure, they got wet, but at least they protected our feet.

While we ran, I thought about everything Rollo the Giant had told us about The Nightmare Novel and this strange world we found ourselves in. And the more I thought about it, the more it really did make sense, although I really didn't know how. I had written the story in *The Nightmare Novel,* not realizing that the characters and creatures I wrote about would actually exist in their own world, a world only in the pages of the book.

Not only that, but because I had written about my family, they were also drawn into this strange nightmare world.

And Rollo made it clear why the wolf had stolen *The Nightmare Novel* from my nightstand: he knew that if I destroyed my story, he would cease to exist.

As crazy as it was, everything made sense. Hannah, my parents, and I were trapped in a world I had created. The only way out was to get *The Nightmare Novel* back and erase my story.

I was determined, but I had no idea what we would be up against. I had no idea where we would find the wolf or what he was capable of. Sure, I had created him, but Rollo the Giant told me that all of the creatures and characters I had made up now had minds of their own. They could turn either good or bad, depending on what they wanted. Unfortunately, it was starting to look like all of the creatures I created were choosing to be bad.

The three of us were soaked as we dashed through the water-filled streets. It was strange: all of the houses were dark, and the street lights were off. I'd never seen the neighborhood in such complete darkness, a blackness deeper than death.

"There," Rollo said. "Up ahead. See?" He pointed above the rooftops, but it was too dark for me to see anything. "There," he said, holding his arm in the same place, still pointing. "Watch."

Suddenly, there was a brilliant flash of lightning, and I could finally see what he was pointing at.

The pirate ship. It was several blocks away.

"But what are we going to do when we get there?" my sister asked.

"We're going to climb aboard," Rollo the Giant replied. "And that's not going to be easy. If they find out that we're after them, the creatures you created will do everything they can to stop us."

We hurried through the dark neighborhood, sloshing through water-filled streets and soaked lawns. Every few seconds, a bolt of lightning would tear across the sky, and we would get a glimpse of the enormous pirate ship. It looked so bizarre, floating through the air.

Just like I saw in my imagination, I thought. *Just like I'd created in my mind.*

We had just about reached the ship, but it was still high in the sky, and I wondered just how we were going to climb aboard.

Suddenly, Rollo stopped walking, and I bumped into him. He turned quickly and looked behind us.

"What?" I asked. "What is it?"

"Quiet," he ordered.

The three of us waited in the rain, looking back in the direction from where we'd just come. I couldn't see much except the silhouettes of houses and the shadows of trees bending in the wind. I was once again struck by how strange and dark everything looked without electricity, without glowing streetlights and lit windows.

But then, I did see something.

Something in the sky.

Something big.

Lightning flashed, and I suddenly realized what was looming in the dark sky, heading right for us.

A dragon.

One of the dragons I had created in my story was only a few houses away, gliding toward us over the rooftops.

Without warning, the dragon opened his mouth, and I knew what was coming next.

Fire.

Oh, there was no doubt about it. I knew this

because that's what I'd created, what I'd written in *The Nightmare Novel*.

Fire-breathing dragons.

"Run!" I shouted, but it was too late. A large yellow plume of white-hot flame was already shooting toward us, and there was no time to run, no way we would be able to get out of its path.

We were about to be cooked.

23

When you are threatened with a life or death situation, your mind reacts without thinking, pushing your body into action. The tongue of fire that was lashing out at us, growing larger as it approached, was inescapable. There was just no way we could outrun it.

So, the three of us did the only thing we could do: we dove down onto the street, which was still gorged with water that almost reached my knees.

In the next instant, I felt the intense heat as it spread out on the water above me. Some of the flames might have even touched my clothing, but I was already soaked, so nothing caught on fire.

Then, the heat was gone. The water had saved us.

I got to my knees as the water in the street rushed around my body. Nearby, Hannah, too, scrambled to her feet, along with Rollo. Above us, the dragon passed by, soaring on his enormous wings, cruising above the houses and trees before vanishing from sight.

"I can't believe that just happened!" Hannah said.

"We're going to have to be very careful," Rollo said. "Things aren't going to get any easier."

He was right, and I knew it. While I didn't understand everything about *The Nightmare Novel,* I did understand this: if we wanted to get out of this world alive, we had to get that book back. I had to get my story back and destroy it.

Which got me to wondering: *could anyone*

destroy the story, or would it have to be me?

"Hey," Hannah said, looking up. "I just noticed something. It stopped raining."

She was right. Although lightning still tore across the sky every few seconds, the rain had stopped.

"It's finally moving on," I said.

Rollo shook his head. "It is gone for now, but it will always be here," he said. "It is what you created, a product of your world."

"But what about other people?" Hannah asked. "How come there aren't other people around?"

"Because I didn't include them in my story," I replied.

Rollo nodded. "You are right. There is no one else in this world except those you have created. No other city exists, either."

"How is that possible?" I asked.

"If we reach the edge of Henderson," the giant said, "you will see that what I say is true. The city ends, and you cannot leave. Remember: the only thing that exists is what you wrote in The Nightmare Novel."

I should have written a happy story about clowns, I thought, or something else that would have been funny. We'd be in a lot less trouble.

Rollo began trudging across the flooded street, and Hannah and I followed. For the most part, Rollo seemed right at home and not too bothered by anything that was going on around him. But I was nervous, and so was my sister. We kept glancing around the dark neighborhood, wondering what might be lurking in the shadows. And because there was no power, none of the streetlights were on and there were no lights on in any of the houses. I'd never seen the city so dark before.

Rollo stepped over the curb and into the grass, which was mostly under water. He stopped and peered warily ahead. Lightning flashed. Thunder rumbled.

"Tell me," he said, "when you wrote your story, did you write about a giant snake?"

"Yes," I replied. "A cobra." A pang of horror jolted my body.

"Well, then," he said calmly. "We'd best not make any sudden moves. He's coming toward us right now."

24

Rollo's words were chilling. Although I couldn't see the snake just yet, I could easily imagine what he looked like, slithering through the darkness, hiding in the shadows. After all, he was a figment of my imagination . . . a figment that had become very, very real.

In the next moment, I didn't have to imagine anymore. The enormous snake's head emerged from around the side of a house, and as he made his way across the wet lawn, I think he was even bigger than I'd created him. His body was as big around as a garbage can, and I was sure he had to be at least thirty feet long or more. What made things even more frightening was that we could see the cobra only when lightning flashed in the sky. I just hoped that he couldn't see us either.

"Don't move a muscle," Rollo repeated quietly. "He doesn't see us, and he's not looking in our direction."

When the lightning flashed, we could see the snake continue to slither across the yard and out into the flooded street, where his body was so big he began to dam up the water. He was so long that we couldn't even see his tail yet, as it was behind the house!

And I knew my sister was absolutely horrified. She didn't like snakes, no matter how big they were. The sight of this giant serpent was probably enough to make her go into shock.

The cobra continued on his way, slithering across yet another yard and behind the house on the opposite side of the street. Lightning continued to flash, and I finally caught a glimpse of his tail. The three of us remained motionless for what seemed like eternity, until the snake could no longer be seen.

"Stay still," Rollo whispered. "Let's wait until he's farther away. He could come back."

We waited for another couple of minutes, then Rollo slowly turned toward us.

"Let's keep going," he said. "Redbeard's ship can't be far."

Hannah and I followed him. We were both frightened about what we might encounter, but Hannah, for the most part, had no idea what we were up against. She didn't know what I had written about, and I hadn't had time to tell her.

"There," Rollo said pointing with his enormous arm. "Up ahead."

Hannah and I stepped around him and looked where he was pointing. In the flashes of lightning, several blocks away, we could see the enormous pirate ship floating through the air, moving through the sky as effortlessly as it would move through an ocean. It looked like an enormous blimp, a hot air balloon sailing above the rooftops.

"But how are we going to get on board?" I asked.

"I don't want to go up there," Hannah said. "Mom and Dad aren't going to like it."

"Mom and Dad are on the ship," I reminded her. "If we don't do something, we're not going to see them again."

"I wish we would've never gone to that garage sale," Hannah said. "I wish you would've never found that notebook, and I wish you would have never written that story."

"You can wish all you want," Rollo said, "but it won't do you any good. Come on."

Rollo started jogging. It seemed easy for him, because of his long legs. Hannah and I had to run as fast as we could just to keep up, and by the time we had reached the pirate ship, we were completely out of breath.

"There's a line dangling," Rollo said. "We

can climb up."

I shook my head. "I'm not very good at climbing," I said

"Me, neither," Hannah said. "And I'm afraid of heights, too."

"Both of you hang on around my neck," Rollo said. "I can pull all three of us up."

And I didn't doubt it, either. Rollo looked like he was as strong as an ox or stronger. I felt safer while he was with us, and I had no idea what we would do without him.

Ahead of us, a long rope dangled from the deck of the pirate ship. It was so long that it dragged on the ground as the ship continued to float through the air. We raced to it.

"Climb up," Rollo said as he knelt down. Hannah and I scaled his back and each of us wrapped a single arm around his huge neck.

"Hang on tight!" he ordered. He picked up the thick line and was about to begin climbing when Hannah suddenly let out a piercing scream. I turned . . . just in time to see the cobra.

He had been following us, waiting for the best time to strike.

That time had come.

25

"Rollo! Climb! Hurry!" I shouted.

Thankfully, Rollo didn't turn around or wait to see what the problem was. He began to climb, hand over hand, up the rope. All Hannah and I could do was hang on as we were lifted off the ground while clinging to the giant.

The cobra struck just as Rollo began climbing. Thankfully, by then, we were off the ground, but the snake still succeeded in biting down on the line. He held it in his mouth and thrashed frantically from side to side. His motions whipped us back and forth, slamming Rollo into the pirate ship. Somehow, he was able to hang on and continue climbing.

The cobra let go of the line and struck out again, but by then, we were too high off the ground, out of his reach. I looked down to see the cobra, with his great hood spread wide and his huge, gaping mouth with two fangs, fall back to Earth.

"That was too close," Hannah said breathlessly. "I thought that thing was going to eat us for sure."

"I bet he would have spit you out," I said. "You probably don't taste very good." I know it wasn't a very nice thing to say, but I guess I was just trying to make a joke to lighten up what was happening.

"Ha ha ha," Hannah replied, her voice heavy with sarcasm. "Very funny."

Rollo continued to climb, and I was amazed at how strong he was. Each of his arms was as big around as my waist, and his powerful muscles worked to pull us higher and higher along the hull of the pirate ship. When we were almost to the top, he stopped. Rollo hung in the air, dangling on the line, while Hannah and I had our arms wrapped firmly around his huge neck.

"Okay," he whispered. *"Keep your eye out. I have no idea what we're going to find when we climb over the railing and reach the deck."*

"What if that mean pirate is there?" Hannah asked.

"Oh, I'm sure he'll be around," Rollo said. "Devon, when you wrote your story, you really created some nasty characters."

Once again, I found myself thinking that this entire situation was all my fault. If I hadn't bought that notebook at the garage sale, if I hadn't dreamed up and written the story, none of this would be happening. I would be in bed, asleep, dreaming of race cars or water parks or something else cool.

On the other hand, I had no idea that what

I was going to write about would come true. I kept trying to tell myself that. If I would've known that my story was going to come to life, I would've written something completely different.

"Here we go," said Rollo, and he began to climb. When we reached the railing, he grabbed it with one hand. Then, he let go of the rope and grabbed the railing with that hand. Slowly, as if he was performing a chin up, he pulled and raised his head over the railing, just enough so he could see. Then, he turned his head toward me.

"Nobody in sight," he whispered. "I am going to pull us over the railing and onto the deck. When we are on board, follow me, stay close, and keep quiet."

It was an odd time to notice it, but I suddenly realized that the lightning had stopped flashing and the thunder wasn't rumbling anymore. Above, the thick, muscular clouds were breaking, and the nickel-plated moon shined through them.

Rollo hoisted us over the railing and gave us

time to climb over his shoulders and onto the deck before he pulled himself over. He stood, and the three of us were now on the deck of the moonlit pirate ship.

"They're all here," Rollo said. "All the characters you wrote about are somewhere on this ship, except the snake and the dragons, which, I'm sure, are not very far away."

"What about the wolf?" I asked quietly. "He's the one who stole my notebook with the story."

"Sooner or later," Rollo whispered back, "we're going to have to find him. He stole your notebook for a reason. He knows that if you get it back, his existence will end, and he is going to do everything in his power to stop us."

"But what about Mom and Dad?" Hannah asked. "What's going to happen to them?"

"If we can get that book back, if we can erase your story or write the ending, your parents will be fine," Rollo replied.

Hannah suddenly swung her arm up and

over her head and swept it frantically back and forth. "There's a bat trying to get me," she said.

I turned and looked up and saw something small flitting in the dull moonlight. It swooped down toward me, and I ducked to get out of its way. When I looked back up, I suddenly realized what it was.

"That's not a bat!" I said. "That's the evil dust fairy that I created in my story! Everybody run!"

My warning came too late. The fairy was just above us, and in the moonlight, I could see her motion with her arms. Suddenly, the air above us was filled with a glittering, powdery substance, and I knew that our adventure had come to an end. The glittery powder would mean we'd be turned to stone, and it was far too late to do anything about it now.

26

It was Rollo who saved us all.

With a powerful sweep of his enormous arm, he lashed out and sent both Hannah and me sprawling across the deck of the pirate ship. I landed on my shoulder and felt a jab of pain. Hannah hit her back and cried out. There was a large tumbling sound, thumping and bumping, as Rollo leapt out of the way.

I rolled over on my side just in time to see the glittering dust fall to the deck. It seemed like a miracle, as I was certain there was no hope of escape. Now we had another chance . . . but we would have to act fast.

Rollo wasted no time. He leapt to his feet.

"Follow me!" he ordered, and he ran across the deck, his boots thumping on the heavy wood. I was worried that he was making too much noise, that he would attract attention, but there really wasn't much else we could do. If we stayed where we were, we would be at the mercy of the evil dust fairy. And if she was anything like I had written in my book, she wasn't going to give up easily.

I helped Hannah to her feet. She was out of breath, gasping and wheezing. When she'd hit the deck, the wind had been knocked from her lungs.

"Come on, Hannah!" I said.

"I . . . can't . . . catch . . . my . . . my . . . breath," Hannah gasped.

"You have to!" I said. "If we don't run, the evil dust fairy is going to come after us again!"

"The eve . . . evil . . . evil . . . dust fairy?!?!" she wheezed.

I didn't have time to explain. Instead, I grabbed her by the hand, helped her to her feet, and pulled her across the deck. Somehow, she managed to draw enough breath to run, although she couldn't move very fast.

Ahead of us, Rollo had vanished into an open doorway that led to the ship's berth . . . which meant that he was going down into the pirate ship.

And we were, too.

I shot a glance over my shoulder and looked up. The evil dust fairy was coming after us, but I knew that if we hurried, we could make it through the doorway where I could close the door and keep her out.

Suddenly, everything seemed so silly that I almost laughed. An evil dust fairy? A pirate ship that flew through the air? A pirate named Redbeard? As Hannah and I ran across the deck, I almost started giggling. The sudden thought of my characters coming to life was somehow incredibly funny.

We reached the doorway that led into the ship's berth. Bursting through it, I pushed Hannah to the side and quickly slammed the door. Then, I slumped against it to catch my breath. Beside me, in the darkness, Hannah was breathing heavily, too. She was still out of breath, but we were both safe.

But not for long.

27

We waited in the darkness. I could hear my heart pounding and Hannah breathing, but nothing else. I listened for any sounds that might come from the ship, but I didn't hear anything.

Gradually, my eyes became accustomed to the dark, and I could make out a faint stairway in the dim surroundings. Obviously, this is where Rollo had gone.

But where was he? He must've gone down the stairs, but I didn't see or hear him.

On top of that, I had never been on a ship before. The only water vessels I had been on were a canoe and a small rowboat. Now, we were on a huge pirate ship, about to go below deck. There was no doubt that there were many passages and rooms, and the possibility of getting lost only added to my growing list of fears.

"What now?" Hannah asked.

"I don't know," I replied. "Maybe we should just wait here. I don't know where Rollo went, but maybe he'll come back."

"I hope he comes back with your book," Hannah said. "I want this nightmare to be over."

"You and me both," I said.

We waited. And waited. Finally, after nearly five minutes, Rollo had not returned. I decided that it would be best if we tried to find him.

"Come on," I said to Hannah. "Let's find Rollo. He's here in the ship somewhere."

"Maybe we'll find Mom and Dad," Hannah said.

"Them, too," I said, and I started thinking

about how confused and scared they must be. After all: a pirate had kidnapped them from their bedroom and sailed away in a ship that floated in the air! They probably were thinking that they'd both gone crazy.

Slowly, we descended the stairs. Because we had slippers on, our feet didn't make any noise. Which was a good thing, because I knew that we needed to move about undetected. We might encounter any one of the creatures I'd written about in my story at any moment.

But most of all, I hoped to find Rollo. He was big and strong, and he seemed to know what to do. He was the one who was going to help us get out of this mess. He could help us find *The Nightmare Novel*. Then, I could erase my story and everything would go back to normal.

I hoped.

But where did Rollo go? I wondered. He must be somewhere on the ship.

We continued tiptoeing carefully down the steps until we came to a room. It was dark and gloomy, and there were no lights. On the far side of the room was the dark, shadowy rectangle of yet another doorway.

"Where did he go?" Hannah asked.

"He's got to be down here somewhere," I replied. "Let's keep going."

We moved silently across the floor, being careful not to make any noise. When we reached the dark doorway, we paused. It appeared to be a hallway of some sort, but it was so dark, I couldn't be sure.

"I'm scared," Hannah whispered.

"I'm not all that thrilled myself," I replied quietly. "But we don't have any other choice. We have to get that book back, and we have to rescue Mom and Dad."

Ahead, I suddenly saw a faint glimmer of light. It appeared to be coming from a room off to the right side of the hallway. We stopped, and I whispered into Hannah's ear.

"There's a light of some sort up there," I said. "Do you see it?"

"Yes," Hannah replied.

"Follow me," I said. "Go slow and be quiet."

Our movements were slow and cautious. We pressed up against the wall until we reached the open doorway. Now that we were closer, I could see that the light was actually a single candle burning on a table. And on the table—

The notebook!

The Nightmare Novel sat on the table, next to the candle! It was in plain sight! I could see the glow of the gold lettering on the cover, illuminated by the flickering flame.

I was so excited to see it that I darted through the doorway and raced toward it, thinking the room was empty.

It wasn't, but it was too late when I realized I'd made a big mistake.

I'd walked right into a trap.

Before I had even picked up the book from the table, I heard a loud bang behind me. The door closed . . . and standing next to it was the wolf!

28

He was just as scary and hideous as I'd remembered him to be. Even more so, now that I was trapped in the room with him.

I heard the doorknob rattle. From the other side of the door, I could hear Hannah's voice.

"Devon? Devon, what happened?" The doorknob rattled again and the door shook, but it wouldn't open.

"She can't help you now," the wolf hissed. "You're all alone."

In the glow of the candle, the wolf looked more menacing, more hideous than ever. It brought back a flood of bad memories, back from the time when I was having those awful nightmares.

"What . . . what do . . . do . . . what do you want with me?" I stammered, backing up against the wall near the table.

"Simple," the wolf sneered. "I want to exist. Now that you have created me, I don't want to go away."

"But I created you from my nightmares and my imagination," I said. "You're not even real."

The wolf nodded. His lips parted, forming a wicked grin that showed his sharp teeth. "Oh, that's not so," he said. "I'm very real thanks to your imagination."

"What have you done with my parents?"

"Oh, Redbeard has them around here somewhere," the wolf replied. "I'm sure they're fine . . . for now."

Then, he tilted his head back and laughed.

It was a howling, snarling laugh, and I covered my ears with my hands to push the insane laughter from my head.

Then, I saw the book on the table and had an idea.

I looked at the space at the bottom of the door. There was a dark line, a shadow, with the space of about an inch.

I looked at the book again.

If I can get the book under that door, I thought, Hannah can pick it up. She can get away with the notebook.

I didn't know if it would work, but I knew one thing: it would throw a monkey wrench into the wolf's plans. He thought that by trapping me in the room, he would be able to stop me once and for all. But if I was able to get the book to Hannah, the wolf would have no reason to hold me hostage anymore.

Quickly, I grabbed the book, bent down, and slid it across the floor. It made an odd zipping sound as the cover scraped along the wood.

The wolf, seeing what I was doing, charged for the book . . . but it was too late. The book skirted across the floor and slid beneath the door, where it vanished.

"Hannah!" I shouted. *"I just shoved the book underneath the door! Pick it up! Run!"*

The wolf did exactly what I had expected: he ran to the door and threw it open. I had hoped Hannah would have time to pick up the book and get away, but it wasn't Hannah on the other side of the door.

It was the zombie.

He was standing in the doorway, holding *The Nightmare Novel* in one hand, grinning wickedly.

"Not so fast," he said in a voice that sounded old and raspy. "You're not going anywhere. As a matter of fact, you're going to stay with us forever and ever, and ever."

29

I was really backed into a corner this time. Not only was I trapped in a room with the wolf, but now the zombie filled the doorway.

And I had no idea where Hannah was or what had happened to her. I hoped she had been able to get away.

Still, I was alone, and I was in a lot of trouble. There was only one thing I could do.

I know it was crazy to even attempt it, but I wasn't just going to stand there and do nothing. If

I did something completely unexpected, something crazy, maybe I would have a fighting chance.

So, I darted across the room. Using all of my body weight, I slammed into the zombie creature. In the process, I snatched The Nightmare Novel from his hand.

I don't consider myself a very lucky person. I've never won anything, and I don't think lucky things happen to me very often.

This time, however, luck was on my side. Somehow, I caught the zombie off-balance. He tumbled back from the weight of my body and fell to the floor. My tactic worked. He had expected me to be too frightened, and he hadn't expected me to charge him.

And I certainly wasn't going to wait around to see what was happening next. Holding onto the book, I leapt over the zombie and bounded up the stairs. My plan was to return to the deck, hoping that the evil dust fairy was gone.

But I still had another problem: I had no pencil, which meant I had no pencil eraser. How was I going to erase my story without an eraser? How would I destroy my story?

I climbed the stairs in the darkness and found the door. I pulled it open and emerged onto the deck. By now, all the clouds were gone, and the full moon shined down brightly. Stars littered the heavens. It was still difficult to see, but the full moon made it much easier.

Frantically, I scanned the deck and the sky above for any signs of the evil dust fairy. I didn't see her.

"Hannah?" I called out. There was no answer.

I wonder what would happen if I destroyed the book? I thought. What if I ripped out the pages and crumpled them up? If I destroyed the pages, would that be the same as erasing the words I'd written?

The wolf and the zombie weren't following me . . . yet. I had no idea where my parents or my sister were, but I figured the best way of saving them would be to destroy my story.

Without wasting another moment, I opened *The Nightmare Novel*. I grabbed the first page and was just about to tear it out when I heard a distinct sound behind me.

The scrape of metal against metal.

I turned to see yet another one of my creations, only a few feet away on the moonlit deck.

The knight in shining armor.

His sword was drawn, and he was ready for battle.

Not only was he ready for battle, but he was looking for it. He pointed the sword at me, lowered his head, leaned forward . . . and lunged! I was going to be shish-kabobbed by a creation from my own imagination!

30

Once again, I was forced to act fast.

The knight wasn't far from me, but I had the advantage of being smaller and quicker, especially because I wasn't wearing a suit of armor.

I darted to the left just in time. The sword missed me by nearly a foot. The knight, however, wasn't able to stop himself and went flying past me.

Carrying the book, I raced along the deck near the ship's railing. I was glad the clouds were gone and the moon was out, as it was much easier to see than when the lightning was flashing.

But I wasn't sure where I was going, or where I should head. There were huge ropes coiled and piled in different places, boxes stacked . . . all sorts of stuff. I was looking for a place to hide and to stay out of sight long enough to tear out the pages of *The Nightmare Novel*.

Behind me, I could hear the knight's armor clanging as he followed me. Yet, I didn't find any place to hide . . . until I looked up. At the top of one of the tall masts was what looked like a large cup, big enough for a man. It occurred to me that I did know something about ships. I knew enough to know that what I was seeing was called a crow's nest, and it was used by sailors to see great distances. They would climb the mast and sit in the crow's nest and look off into the horizon.

That's it! I thought. There's no way that dude in his heavy armor will be able to follow me if I can climb up the mast.

Either way, I had to quickly make a decision,

because the knight was showing no signs of slowing down.

I raced to the mast, where I found a rope ladder dangling.

More luck! I thought. Climbing the rope ladder was going to be much easier than climbing the mast.

I tucked *The Nightmare Novel* beneath my arm and started scrambling up the rope ladder. It was difficult at first, because it wasn't like a wooden or aluminum ladder that was solid and firm. The rope ladder wiggled with every movement, but I quickly got the hang of it.

The trouble was that the knight had the same idea. He had sheathed his sword and began climbing the ladder, although he was much slower than me. Still, if he kept coming, sooner or later he would reach the crow's nest, and there was nowhere I could go.

If I can get to the top in time, I thought, I might find a way to cut the ladder or untie it from inside the crow's nest.

So, I kept climbing, focusing my attention on making it to the crow's nest as fast as I could, careful to keep The Nightmare Novel tucked beneath my arm so I wouldn't lose it.

And I might even be able to tear out the pages of the book before the knight reaches me anyway, I thought. *If I could do that, maybe this whole nightmare would be over.*

While I climbed, I wondered what would happen when I destroyed the book. Would I suddenly wake up in bed, only to find that everything had been a bad dream? Rollo hadn't been clear about that. There was still so much about the book that I didn't understand.

I reached the crow's nest and climbed inside. There was plenty of room to move around, but it was quickly apparent that I'd have to do something about the knight in armor, as he was climbing the rope ladder much faster than I'd expected.

At first, I tried to untie it, but the knots were too tight. I looked around for something to cut the ropes with, but there was nothing.

Panic began to set in as the knight climbed higher and higher, closer and closer to the crow's nest. Another few feet and he would be upon me.

Two shadows suddenly appeared on the deck far below.

Rollo and Hannah!

They emerged from the door that led into the ship's berth. Of course, all I could see of them were their dark silhouettes, but in the moonlight, I could see enough of their features to know who they were.

"Rollo!" I shouted down. "I'm up here! Help!"

Rollo raced to the mast, and my sister followed. When he looked up and saw what was happening, he grabbed the rope and began shaking it. This caused the ladder to twist and turn frantically, and the knight could no longer climb, as he had to use all of his strength just to hang on.

"Rollo!" I shouted again. I held up *The Nightmare Novel* for him to see, although I wasn't sure he'd be able to see it from so high up.

"I have The Nightmare Novel!" I continued. "What will happen if I tear the pages out?!?!"

"I don't know!" his voiced boomed back.

"Well, I'm going to try it!" I shouted.

Suddenly, I saw more motion below me. On the deck, more figures were appearing.

Mom and Dad!

But still others emerged from the ship's berth. I saw the pirate, Redbeard, along with the wolf and the zombie. Even the evil dust fairy appeared, swooping far below like a crazed bat.

But what was far worse were the dragons. They appeared out of nowhere, flying at incredible speeds. The first one flew just over the mast, and he blocked out the moonlight when he went by.

The other dragon was flying lower, and he was coming toward me. However, at the very last moment, he dove down. When I realized what he was doing, it was far too late.

His wing slammed into the mast, snapping it in two. I lost my grip on The Nightmare Novel, and it went sailing into the air. And even worse: I was sent tumbling out of the crow's nest, flailing my arms and legs like a madman, in a free fall. I was either going to hit the deck of the ship or tumble to the earth below where I would slam into the ground or the roof of a house.

Either way, I knew one thing for sure: there was no way I'd be able to survive the fall.

31

As I tumbled through the air, all I could think about was the pain I would feel when I finally struck the deck or the ground, or whatever I was going to hit. Maybe I would hit so hard that I wouldn't feel a thing. It would be a painless death, over in less than one second.

And the screaming! Hannah and my mom were screaming their heads off. I'm sure they felt terrible, knowing there was nothing they could do.

My vision spun around and around as my

body twisted and turned. One instant I caught a glimpse of the silvery moon; the next instant, I saw the figures on the deck of the pirate ship below. They were coming faster and faster as I continued to fall.

Finally, in the instant just before I hit, I saw the moon for what I knew would be the last time. I closed my eyes just before my body slammed into the deck.

But wait a minute! I hadn't hit anything hard. In fact, I wasn't in any pain at all!

I opened my eyes to find Rollo staring down at me. He had caught me in his huge arms and prevented me from hitting the deck! He had saved my life!

I heard a thump nearby and glanced down to see *The Nightmare Novel*. It had smacked the deck hard and tumbled a couple of times before stopping.

The scene around me quickly became chaotic. Everyone was making a mad dash for the book, except, of course, my parents and my sister.

Rollo, however, was closest to the book. As he set me down, he kicked it away from the wolf, who was nearly upon it.

And that's when I sprang. I darted around the wolf and ran to *The Nightmare Novel*. This time, I wasn't going to waste any time at all. I flipped open the book and began tearing out the pages as quickly as I could, tossing them into the air, tearing and ripping. Creamy white pages tumbled into the air and fell around me like leaves. I pulled furiously, violently, page after page after page.

My surroundings began to change, and it was so sudden that I almost stopped ripping out the pages so I could witness what was going on.

Everything around me began to fade. Things became fuzzy and colorless. In the light of the moon, I had been able to make out various colors and hues; now, everything had a black and white tone, like an old photograph.

And the creatures! Although they were still moving, they were beginning to vanish right before my very eyes. The two dragons in the sky had returned, circling high above. They, too, appeared to be fading away like smoky clouds. So were my parents and my sister. Still, I continued tearing out the pages of *The Nightmare Novel* until there was nothing left but the front and back cover and the spine.

Everything around me had faded into nothing, and I was immersed in darkness. I couldn't even see *The Nightmare Novel* in my hands. I felt strange: lightheaded and weak. My legs suddenly became incredibly weary, and I knew that I wasn't going to be able to stand for much longer.

What's happening? I thought. *Have I done something wrong?*

I had destroyed *The Nightmare Novel*, but in doing so, had I only made things worse?

Then, my legs couldn't hold me any longer; I felt my body collapsing, and I figured I had done something horribly wrong. That was the last thought I had before my mind went blank.

32

When I came to, I was completely confused.

Where am I? I wondered. *What had happened?*

Most scary of all, however, was when I opened my eyes only to find that I was still surrounded by darkness. It was scary.

Why can't I see? And again, Where am I? Is this what it's like to be dead?

Then, I heard a noise that sounded distinctly like a pan being dropped into a kitchen sink.

Someone coughed.

What's going on?

I shifted and moved and quickly found my answer.

I was in my bed, under the covers. That's why I couldn't see anything.

Silly.

I pulled down the covers, overjoyed to see the familiar sight of my bedroom.

Had it all been a dream? Was everything that I had experienced only a nightmare?

I sat up in bed and looked around my room. Everything seemed the same, except for one thing.

My notebook. *The Nightmare Novel.* I had gone to bed with it sitting on my nightstand. Now, it was gone. The only things on my nightstand were my clock radio, my lamp, and my pen.

I looked on the floor.

Nothing.

I slipped out of bed and looked beneath it.

Nope. Not there.

I walked around my bedroom, searching. I

didn't find it anywhere.

If everything that had happened was only in my nightmare, then where did the notebook go? It should have been on my nightstand, where I had left it the night before. And I was certain that neither Hannah nor my parents would have come into my room and taken it.

I stood in the middle of my bedroom for a moment, completely puzzled. I thought about the experiences I had during the night. What had happened didn't seem like a dream or nightmare, as it was very clear in my mind. Usually, when you wake up from a dream, it's hazy and fuzzy. My memory of what had happened was crisp and clear.

I left my bedroom and walked into the kitchen. I smelled coffee and toast. Mom was putting some dishes into the sink, and Dad had just pulled two mugs from the cupboard. When Mom saw me, she spoke.

"There you are, Sleepyhead," she said. "You really slept in this morning."

"Did anyone come in my bedroom and take my notebook?" I asked. I knew what the answer was going to be, and I was right.

"We didn't," Dad replied as he shook his head.

"How about Hannah?" I asked.

Mom shook her head. "Your sister is still sleeping. In fact, go wake her up and tell her breakfast will be ready soon. Then, I'll tell you about the crazy dreams your father and I had last night."

I froze and looked at her. "Crazy dreams?"

"Awful," Dad said. "But the craziest part was that your mother and I both had the exact same dream."

Hannah appeared in the hallway, wearing her pink nightgown and white slippers. Her hair looked like a rat's nest.

"Did you say something about dreams?" she asked. "Because I had the freakiest nightmare of my life last night." She yawned and rubbed her eyes.

"Let me guess," I said. "Everybody dreamed about a pirate ship. Mom and Dad, you dreamed that you were kidnapped by a pirate named Redbeard, didn't you?"

Mom and Dad looked stunned.

"How did you know?" Dad asked.

"And there was a zombie on the ship, and a wolf. And a little tiny fairy buzzing around."

Mom and Dad continued to stare at me.

"You had the same dream?" Mom asked.

"I had the same dream, too," Hannah said.

"I've never heard of anything like this before," Dad said. He looked at Mom. "How can that happen?"

"It happened because I wrote about it in The Nightmare Novel," I replied. I explained how I had written the story, and how the creatures had come to life.

"Are you telling us that your story became real?" Dad asked.

I shook my head. "No," I said. "My story didn't come alive. The characters did. The characters all had minds of their own. When I created them, they came alive. The only way to get rid of them was to destroy The Nightmare Novel."

"I'm not understanding any of this," Mom said.

"I don't understand any of it, either," I said.

"And I don't believe it," Dad said. "You can't make creatures come alive by writing about them in a book."

"But how else can we explain everyone having the same dream?" Hannah asked.

"I don't know," Dad replied. "All I know is it was an awful dream. Yes, it's weird that we all experienced it. But that's all it was. A dream. A nightmare."

And that was pretty much the end of it. We talked about it a little bit over the course of the day, but my parents wouldn't believe that it was anything but a dream.

As for me? I had another problem. I'd worked really hard on my story, and now it was gone. I would have to write it all over again.

Later in the afternoon, I got started. But it occurred to me that what had happened in my dream last night was better than my original story. So, instead of rewriting the story, I simply wrote about what had happened last night. Dream or no dream, it was a pretty horrifying experience, and I thought it would make a great story. But I kept the title, because I thought it was cool. The only thing I added to it was my home state.

The Nevada Nightmare Novel.

My teacher, Mr. Harper, was impressed. He loved *The Nevada Nightmare Novel*, and he gave me an 'A.' He said it was the best story I've ever written. In fact, Mr. Harper asked me to read the entire story, out loud, to the class. I had never done anything like that before, so I was a little nervous. But my classmates really seemed to enjoy the story. Everyone said it was the weirdest story they'd ever heard. Of course, I didn't tell them that the events in my story had actually happened. I just told them it was a story I had made up. That seemed like the easiest thing to do. Besides: I didn't want my classmates thinking I was crazy.

I was walking home from school that day, feeling very proud of myself. I had written a great story, and I had read it out loud in front of the entire class. That made me feel good.

"Hey, Devon," a voice from behind me said.

I stopped and turned around. It was a girl in my class. She was new, and I didn't know what her name was. She was about my height with very long, black hair.

"I liked your story," she said. "It was really scary."

"Thank you," I replied.

"Do you like to write?" she asked.

"Yeah," I said, nodding my head. "I like it a lot."

"So do I," she said. "I write all the time. In fact, I just finished writing a story about something that happened to me last winter before we moved."

"Where did you move from?" I asked.

"Idaho," she said.

"I've never been there," I said.

"It's a great place," the girl said. "But something happened to me last winter that still gives me chills."

"Is that what you wrote about?" I asked.

She nodded. "Yes," she replied. "Would you like to read it?"

"Sure," I said.

The girl slipped off her backpack and unzipped it. She pulled out a thick notebook.

"Wow," I said. "That's a long story."

"And every word of it is true," she said.

I looked at the cover and read the title.

Idaho Ice Beast, by Jessica Dutton.

I looked up at the girl and raised an eyebrow. "This is a true story?" I asked.

"Yeah," she said. "But I don't expect you to believe it."

"Why?" I asked.

"Because it's just too crazy," Jessica said. "In fact, everyone who has read it thinks I made it up. They don't think it's real."

"Can I take it home and give it back to you when I'm done?" I asked.

Jessica nodded. "Sure," she said. "I'd like to know what you think about it."

Continuing home, I began to read her story. It was very interesting, and very well written.

But it can't be true, I thought. There's no way it could be true . . . because what she had written was one of the most terrifying stories I'd ever read.

Next:

#32: Idaho
Ice
Beast

Continue on for
a FREE preview!

"Jessica, Mom says if you don't get out of bed right now, you're not going on the trip!"

Those words were spoken by my little brother, who had opened my bedroom door and was peeking inside.

"Get out of my room, Garrett," I said from beneath the covers. I had no idea what time it was, but I was tired. Oh, I was excited for the trip and all that, which was the reason I couldn't get to sleep the night before. Which, of course was the reason I hadn't gotten out of bed when my alarm went off. I just hit the snooze button and covered my head with my pillow. I was so tired, and all I wanted was a little more sleep.

But I knew it wasn't going to happen. We were headed for Sun Valley for a ski trip, and I knew I had to get up and get ready. Most of my things were already packed, so I didn't have too much more to do.

And even though I was tired, I really was excited. Every winter, my family travels from our home in Boise, Idaho, to Sun Valley, Idaho, where we stay at a lodge for a week. We ski, snowshoe, snowboard, ride inner tubes down hills . . . it's a week of great fun. I've always loved the winter, and I always look forward to our trip to Sun Valley.

But there's something else about Sun Valley that's always fascinated me:

Bigfoot. The abominable snowman. Yeti. Sasquatch. Or whatever you want to call him. Some people who've seen the creature around Sun

Valley call him the ice beast.

Now, before you think I'm totally crazy, you need to know that I don't actually believe in the monster. But many people do, and I like to think that, somewhere in the mountains, maybe a bigfoot creature really does exist. After all, many people have claimed to have seen Bigfoot, and some people have even taken pictures. All of the pictures are either blurry or out of focus, so you never really get a good look at the beast. But it's fun to think about, and I often wondered if such a creature really does exist, hiding in the mountains somewhere.

I had no idea that I was about to get my answer, and I certainly had no idea that our fun vacation was going to turn into such a terrifying experience that would change my life forever.

It took me a while, but I finally dragged myself out of bed and into the kitchen. I was so tired that I forgot to put on my slippers.

"I was just coming to get you," Mom said. "I thought you were going to sleep forever."

"I couldn't get to sleep last night," I replied with a yawn. "I kept thinking about our trip and how much fun we are going to have, even though I knew I needed to get to sleep. I am so tired." I yawned again as I covered my mouth with my hand.

"Well," Mom said, "maybe you can sleep in the car for a little while. It's a three-hour drive to Sun Valley, but it will take us a little longer this time because we're picking up your cousins."

That got me even more excited. Our cousins live in Mountain Home, which is a city in Idaho, south of Boise. To get to Sun Valley, we have to go through Mountain Home, and this year our cousins would be joining us on our vacation. My favorite cousin is Isaac. He is twelve years old, just like me. In fact, our birthdays are only a couple of weeks apart. He loves to do a lot of the same things that I do, and I knew we would have a great time at the resort in Sun Valley.

I wolfed down a bowl of cereal, got dressed, packed the rest of my things, and was finally ready to go. Dad, Mom, Garrett and I piled into the car, and we were on our way by seven o'clock. Dad insisted that we get started early, so we could get to Sun Valley before noon. That way, he said, we'd have the rest of the day to ski.

I slept all the way to Mountain Home. Garrett brought a book with him, so he kept busy reading and didn't bug me. When we made it to our cousin's house, they were ready to go. Isaac rode with us; the rest of his family followed us in their vehicle, and we drove the rest of the way to the resort at Sun Valley.

It was in the lobby of the resort where I first had an indication that our week-long trip wasn't going to be near as fun as I'd imagined.

Dad was at the front desk, getting checked in. We'd hauled all of our gear inside and placed it on a cart so we wouldn't have to drag any of it up stairs or on an elevator. My mom and my aunt and uncle stood nearby, chatting.

"Hey," Isaac said as he picked up a newspaper from a coffee table by the fireplace. "Check this out!"

He held out the newspaper. On the front was a blurry, black and white photograph that appeared to show some sort of creature hiding among trees, boulders, and snow.

"Is this the Idaho Ice Beast?" I read the headline aloud.

"It looks like some sort of white bigfoot creature," Isaac said. "It says he was spotted not far from here."

"It's not real," I said. "There's no such thing."

Isaac shook his head. "Yes, there is," he said. "But he stays hidden in the mountains so not many people see him. Wouldn't it be cool to see him during our vacation?"

"Sure," I said, "if he was real. But he's not real, and that picture is a fake."

I continued staring at the picture. Yes, it looked like some sort of creature was peering out between snow-covered pine trees, but it could have been just a trick of light and shadow, and I didn't believe for a minute that it was actually some sort of creature.

Yet, something about the picture made me feel uneasy. I didn't believe it was a real creature, but the more I stared at it, the more anxious I became.

What if there really is some sort of weird creature out there? I thought. *What if he hunts people? What if his favorite snack is kids on snowshoes or skis?*

I can be that way, sometimes. Sometimes, I allow my imagination run wild, and I get freaked out.

Well, I was going to get freaked out on our vacation, for sure . . . but it would have nothing to do with my imagination.

The rest of the day was a lot of fun. After we loaded everything into our room, we ate lunch with my cousins and my aunt and uncle in the restaurant at the resort. I sat with Isaac, and we talked and laughed the entire time. He really is pretty cool, and I wished he lived closer to our home in Boise, because we only get to see each other a couple of times a year.

After lunch, everyone went skiing except for me and Isaac. I like snowboarding better than skiing, and so does Isaac, so that's what we did. I'm not very good at it, but it sure is a lot of fun.

And every so often, while sailing down the hill, I would stare off into the woods and think about the creepy picture from the newspaper. That got me thinking about all the other people who claimed so have seen a bigfoot creature, and I started to wonder again.

What if there really is a creature like that, living in the forest? What if he's watching me, right now.

But these thoughts vanished quickly. I had to pay attention to the hill, to what I was doing so I didn't crash into anything or anyone. Still, I fell a bunch of times, but I didn't get hurt. Actually, it was kind of fun.

That night, we had pizza in our room, which was connected to my cousin's room through a door. We all ate together. Isaac, his little sister Sarah, my little brother Garrett, and I watched a movie. It was good, but I had a hard time keeping my eyes open. After all, I'd hardly slept the night before, and I got sleepy early. I changed into my pajamas and fell asleep on the couch . . . and that's where I was when I woke up some time during the night.

It was dark, and I was confused. There was a window with a curtain drawn, letting in a little light around the edges. It took me a moment to realize where I was.

Oh, yeah, I thought. *We're in Sun Valley, on our trip. I must have fallen asleep.*

The hotel room had two separate bedrooms; one for Garrett and me, and one for my parents. I didn't want to sleep on the couch for the rest of the night, so I slowly stood and walked across the room. The door to Mom and Dad's room was open a tiny bit, and the door to my room was open all the way. There was a tiny nightlight glowing inside, and I could see the lumpy figure of Garrett sleeping beneath the covers on his bed.

I walked into the room. Like the larger living room, our bedroom also had a window. The curtains were closed, but thin bands of sugary light seemed to burn around the edges.

I wonder if it's snowing, I thought, and I tiptoed to the window and drew open the curtain.

Outside, several bright lights lit up the snow covered parking area in the distance. We were on the third floor, so I had a good view of the ski hills, as they, too had a few lights positioned up the mountain. The snow was falling lightly, and I was sure we would get a few inches by morning.

I was just about to let go of the curtain and allow the fall back into place, when I saw something move. Something big, in the shadows near the trees.

I stopped and squinted, trying to see better. *Nothing.*

I continued watching, trying to see what had moved. I saw something, I was sure, but I didn't know what.

Finally, after not seeing it again, I climbed into bed and fell asleep.

The next morning, I awoke well rested, excited, and ready for the day. I had completely forgotten about the thing I'd seen moving during the night . . . Until Isaac and I went downstairs for breakfast.

That's when we saw a police car parked out front of the resort beneath the awning, and I knew something horrible had happened.

When Isaac and I saw the uniformed man and woman in the lobby, we stopped.

"Uh-oh," Isaac whispered. *"Somebody's in trouble."*

It was then that I remembered seeing the strange sight outside the hotel room window last night, and I wondered if that had something to do with the police being there.

I knew I saw something, I thought. *There was something out there last night. Something in the shadows, near the trees.*

"Jessica?" Isaac said. "What's the matter? You look like you've seen a ghost."

"Not a ghost," I said. "But I saw something last night. Something in the snow, outside by the woods."

"What was it?" Isaac asked.

I shrugged. "I'm not really sure," I replied. "It was late, and it was dark. I saw something move, but I didn't really get a good look at what it was."

We started walking again, making our way past the two police officers at the front desk. I wanted to know why they were there, but I didn't want to be nosy. It really wasn't any of my business, but I still wondered if it had anything to do with the strange thing I have seen the night before.

Just what did I see? I wondered again. *I saw something move, I know that much. But it could've been a man, or maybe just a tree branch.*

The restaurant was connected to the lobby,

and Isaac and I walked through a set of double doors. It was still a little early, so there weren't many people having breakfast yet. We chose a table that had enough chairs for everyone in my family and Isaac's, and sat.

Isaac turned his head and looked at the police officers.

"Maybe there was a robbery," Isaac said. "Or maybe there's a crazed killer on the loose!"

A woman came over to our table and smiled, filling up our water glasses.

"Can I get you to something for breakfast?" she said.

"Not yet," I said. We were waiting for our families to join us."

"How come the police are here?" Isaac asked her.

The server turned and looked at the two police officers standing by the front desk in the lobby.

"Oh, that," she said. "No big deal. Someone drove their car into another car in the parking lot.

It's slippery out there today. Nobody got hurt, but one of the cars has a big dent. Whenever that happens, they have to file a police report."

That made sense, and I was glad to hear that it had nothing to do with what I'd seen the night before. I was still a little nervous about the picture I'd seen in the paper the day before, but I quickly forgot about Bigfoot monsters when our families joined us for breakfast.

We made plans for the day. Mom, Dad, and my aunt and uncle were going to ski. Garrett and my cousin, Sarah, were enrolled in a ski class, so they would be busy the entire day.

I had planned on snowboarding, but Isaac showed me something else.

"Look at this," he said, and he pulled a folded brochure from his pocket. It was colorful, and as he unfolded it, I could se that it was a trail map.

"These are snowshoe trails," he said. "Let's rent snowshoes and go for a hike through the hills. We might even see that weird Bigfoot creature that we saw in the newspaper yesterday."

I rolled my eyes. "Yeah, right," I said. "But snowshoeing sounds like it would be a lot of fun. Have you ever done it before?"

" Only once," Isaac replied. "It's great, once you get the hang of it. Snowshoes allow you to walk in snow that is really deep. You can even run while wearing them, but it takes some practice."

"Why would anyone want to run with snowshoes?" I asked.

Isaac shrugged. "Beats me," he said. "I'm not planning on running with my snowshoes on."

"Me neither," I said.

But we were both wrong. Soon, both of us would be running with our snowshoes on . . . but we would be running to save our lives.

ABOUT THE AUTHOR

Johnathan Rand has been called 'one of the most prolific authors of the century.' He has authored more than 75 books since the year 2000, with well over 4 million copies in print. His series include the incredibly popular **AMERICAN CHILLERS**, **MICHIGAN CHILLERS, FREDDIE FERNORTNER, FEARLESS FIRST GRADER,** and **THE ADVENTURE CLUB.** He's also co-authored a novel for teens (with Christopher Knight) entitled **PANDEMIA.** When not traveling, Rand lives in northern Michigan with his wife and three dogs. He is also the only author in the world to have a store that sells only his works: **CHILLERMANIA!** is located in Indian River, Michigan and is open year round. Johnathan Rand is not always at the store, but he has been known to drop by frequently. Find out more at:

www.americanchillers.com

ATTENTION YOUNG AUTHORS!
DON'T MISS

JOHNATHAN RAND'S

AUTHOR QUEST

THE DEFINITIVE WRITER'S CAMP
FOR SERIOUS YOUNG WRITERS

If you want to sharpen your writing skills, become a better writer, and have a blast, Johnathan Rand's Author Quest is for you!

Designed exclusively for young writers, Author Quest is 4 days/3 nights of writing courses, instruction, and classes at Camp Ocqueoc, nestled in the secluded wilds of northern lower Michigan. Oh, there are lots of other fun indoor and outdoor activities, too . . . but the main focus of Author Quest is about becoming an even better writer! Instructors include published authors and (of course!) Johnathan Rand. No matter what kind of writing you enjoy: fiction, non-fiction, fantasy, thriller/horror, humor, mystery, history . . . this camp is designed for writers who have this in common: they LOVE to write, and they want to improve their skills!

For complete details and an application, visit:

www.americanchillers.com

Johnathan Rand travels internationally for school visits and book signings! For booking information, call:

1 (231) 238-0338!

www.americanchillers.com

JOIN THE FREE AMERICAN CHILLERS FAN CLUB!

It's easy to join . . . and best of all, it's FREE!
Find out more today by visiting:

WWW.AMERICANCHILLERS.COM

And don't forget to browse the on-line superstore, where you can order books, hats, shirts, and lots more cool stuff!